Queen of Belize

BOOK 8 OF THE QUEENS OF THE CASTLE SERIES

AIKEN PONDER

Words to Ponder Publishing
Chagrin Falls, Ohio

Address inquiries to Words to Ponder Publishing Company, LLC
eBook ISBN: 978-7358795-8-1
Trade Paperback ISBN: 978-1-941328-58-3

Cover Design by Woodson Creative Studio.
Interior Design by Lissa Woodson

Words to Ponder Publishing Company, LLC
Printed in the United States of America
For more information, visit https://www.florenza.org or
https://www.wordstoponderpublishing.com.

Queen of Belize

BOOK 8 OF THE QUEENS OF THE CASTLE SERIES

AIKEN PONDER

I dedicate this book to my husband, best friend, and soulmate, my Papa Bear. To my children, Jessica, and Missy, who are my first and loudest cheerleaders. To family and friends, who are my most incredible supporters.

To Naleighna Kai and the NK Tribe Called Success for taking me under your wing and teaching this bird to soar. To Stephanie M. Freeman, my "drink and two-step" partner in crime. To my editors, who takes the broken pieces of my words, ensuring they are woven together in such a fashion, they create a beautiful tapestry.

To the beta readers who dedicate countless hours to be the first set of eyes to partake of the deliciousness of this story. To JL Campbell for embracing me during this project and helping my light to not dim. I appreciate you so very much. And to you, the reader, for your encouragement and support of the beautiful gift of writing given to me by God.

Prologue

"Don't kill her," he begged as his hands went up, and the unmistakable stench of fear permeated the air. "Please ... let me live."

Robert's eyes bulged to the point of nearly popping out of the sockets and ricocheting across the living room floor. His amber skin was ashen with terror. "You don't have to do this."

With each tearful plea, he inched ever so slightly to the left.

"Do you really think I'm that stupid?" Her lips curled over her upper teeth. Within nanoseconds, she was in his face spitting out each word. Dirty fingernails chewed down to nubs gripped the handle of the M5. "I know what you're trying to do."

Ironically, the weapon had been a Christmas gift from him.

The thought that he once loved the demon in a meat-suit now standing before him, masquerading as a human, caused bile to rise in the back of his throat and nearly choke him.

How could someone who'd once taken his breath away now want to end his life?

"I know what you're doing." She instantly became judge and jury of his actions. *"Dumb ass. I helped you to retrofit the curio to hold the weapons."*

She kicked several empty moving boxes out of the way as she stomped over and yanked open the top drawer. *"Ah, the .38 Special on steroids. It's still loaded just like I left it."* She thrust the Smith and Wesson .357 Magnum revolver into her belted waistband. *"You won't be needing this."*

Robert immediately dropped to his knees, laced his fingers together, and swayed from side to side trying to contain the excruciating emotional pain. *"Why're you doing this?"* His throat was on fire. Vocal cords felt as though they were being sliced with a white-hot sword. At that moment, he didn't exude the swagger that accompanied being the youngest Black attorney with Appleman, Greenhagen, and Einhorn, LLP; Robert sounded like a television commercial that warned about the dangers of nicotine. *"You already killed my father,"* he moaned.

"Daddy," Ivy Davidson bellowed over her shoulder, loud enough for her voice to carry into the adjacent room. *"Show the good attorney that we mean business with his lady friend."*

Rahul Perez's soiled, steel-toe boots trudged along the hand-scraped teakwood floors. Heavy steps left thick, black scuff marks in his path.

Bam! The bathroom door splintered as it flew completely off the hinges. It bounced against the wall and shattered on the floor removing the sole source of protection for his new bride.

Robert collapsed to the rug, protesting, *"She never did anything to you. Please don't take this out on her. Our marriage was over long before—"*

"Before what?" she seethed. *"Before you tried to steal my babies? Or when you left me homeless?"* Ivy jammed the barrel of the gun so deeply into his left temple, droplets of blood dripped down his face and onto the collar of the linen shirt, instantly turning the white fabric bright red.

He leaped to his feet and lunged at her, attempting to snatch the weapon but lost his footing. His chin smacked against the floor as he *went face down. Ivy struck his head with such force, his teeth rattled. The droplets of blood became a river and gushed uncontrollably. His left eye swelled shut, and his head began to pound.*

Urine drenched his organic cotton khaki shorts, saturating the hand-woven Persian rug.

Her nose wrinkled as she sniffed. "Daddy," she shouted. "The son of a bitch pissed himself." Her laughter was maniacal. "I should kill you right now but witnessing your pain is so much sweeter." She stooped and stared him in the eye. "And, trust me, you will lose everything!"

She whispered in his ear, "Where are my manners?" Her hot, putrid breath invaded his nostrils. "You shouldn't be having all this fun without your fiancé, now, should you?"

She shouted into the next room, "Kick her in the face, Daddy."

Blood-curdling screams reverberated throughout the spacious rooms and bounced off priceless African artifacts. In a previous life, the statues had witnessed unspeakable carnage. Robert brought the relics home from his many excursions in hope that they'd find solace. He had freed them, but who was going to rescue him?

The faint sound of police sirens rang in the distance. "Dammit, Daddy! Get it over with." A string of saliva defied gravity as it dribbled off her chin. "Just put a bullet to the back of her head."

Rahul Perez pulled the trigger of the Glock 19 and fired just as the Westminster Quarters in the grandfather clock marked seven o'clock. Robert's screams exploded from a place so deep within his soul that his heart shattered into a thousand pieces.

"You are next," Ivy warned.

Robert looked up through tears as the bright light of the muzzle flashed nanoseconds before the bullet ripped through his chest. He never saw the second, third, or fourth shot. Robert Davidson fell dead on the floor he had laid with his own hands.

Chapter 1

The excitement from the live audience was electrifying. The buzz of voices rose and fell as camera operators spoke through earbuds to a broadcast technician backstage. Spotlights were adjusted, and makeup artists dashed to the stage, brushes, lipstick, and powder in hand to make the host and guest look their very best.

"Ms. Eituk." A young lady wearing a huge afro held up a makeup brush. Her flawless skin and radiant smile reminded Naysa of a younger version of the American actress Rutina Wesley. She loved her character in the gritty drama True Blood. "May I?"

"Of course," Naysa replied. "You're the expert."

"Thank you for those very kind words," she said.

Thirty seconds later, the director put up two fingers, followed by one, then pointed to the reporter. His paisley necktie was loose at the collar of a coffee-stained, wrinkled white shirt. "And we'll begin in five, four, three."

The host's red curls bounced as she spoke into the lapel microphone. The black silk blouse accented her ample bosom when she leaned forward. "Thank you for tuning in as we interview ordinary people who are doing extraordinary things. Joining us today is Ms. Naysa Eituk."

The camera panned to Naysa, and she looked through the lens as if she was face to face with the television audience.

"Ms. Eituk has exciting news she'd like to share with us," the reporter announced.

Connecting with the people was Naysa's superpower. As a citizen, she was in touch with the concerns of Belizeans. This brought high praises from most, but not all. Her ears were tuned in to those who'd lost their voice. She boldly spoke what they feared to whisper.

The reporter fingered a stray curl and placed it behind her ear. "But first, we have the weather updates from meteorologist John Kressley." She turned her head slightly to the left. "Take it away, John."

"Thank you, Vanya. Happy Independence Day, everyone." He clicked the handheld device which controlled the images that only appeared on the monitor situated offstage. As he spoke about the heatwave forecasted next week, many audience members never took their eyes off Naysa.

"That's the report for the next ten days," he said. "We'll return following this short commercial break."

While the meteorologist chattered on, Naysa glanced at Ian, positioned at the far end of the room. The suit perfectly hugged his six-foot four-inch muscular frame. He sat quietly, observing everyone. Seven other well-built men in identical tailor-made suits were scattered throughout the audience. They were recently redirected from their duties at the Castle to protect Naysa and Luiza. Naysa's vehement protests that she was more than capable of providing her own security fell on deaf ears. After an unknown assailant shot into their residence, Khalil Germaine, her godfather, and head of the Castle, overrode her objections. To her dismay, Ian Richardson was sent.

Godfather, did you have to send him? It could've been anyone but him.

Today, they were on elevated alert. The number of those in attendance was higher than the information given during the briefing. Plus, those in opposition to Naysa's mission never rested from their protests and attempts at sabotage.

Naysa panned the audience, then connected with Ian's steel-blue eyes and raised an eyebrow.

Ian nodded, a sure sign he'd made a mental note to check into the inconsistency.

Naysa praised her security team daily for allowing her to stay visible while at the same time feeling protected. The hardest adjustment she'd had to make in her drive to rebuild and protect the coral reefs was being constantly surrounded by men carrying guns. She dared not complain. Especially not to the very ones who stood between her and a bullet. She wished someone had been as diligent for her mother.

Maybe she wouldn't have ended up in a wheelchair because of a crazed female bent on revenge. Thank God she'd made it through the horror of that attempt on her life. Her father hadn't been as lucky.

Chapter 2

After the thirty-second break, a young man in a white polo shirt with the station's logo carried a microphone to an older female situated on the front row.

She cleared her throat then folded a slip of paper she'd been reading before speaking. "Ms. Eituk, I've heard a major cruise line is developing on one of our islands and plans to divert tourists there rather than to our southern shores."

A chorus of whispers rose from the audience.

In a strident tone, she added, "Our island depends upon those tourist dollars."

The stage assistant attempted to pull the microphone away, but she raised her index finger, indicating she wasn't done with her question.

Ian took a few steps forward and stood beneath the elevated cameraman's chair.

"If a new port does develop, what can be done to ensure they don't divert all ships there instead of here?" She then relinquished the microphone with a sharp nod, emboldened by the applause and pats on the back as she reclaimed the seat.

"Thank you for your question," Naysa responded, watching Ian move from the center of the aisle to sit a row behind the woman. "I didn't get your name."

She blinked several times rapidly then chewed the inside of her lower lip. "Angel," she finally said. "Angelica Norman."

"Ah, Messenger of God," Naysa said, acknowledging the meaning of her name. "Ms. Norman. I'm mindful that development has begun on one of our smaller islands. Please know, this will not hinder—"

"We'll be back in five, four, three," the announcer said as he counted down his fingers. When he got to one, he pointed to the reporter.

"Welcome back," Vanya said in a voice that had been perfected from hours of training. Focusing on Naysa, she said, "You have achieved a lot in terms of your education."

She listed Naysa's qualifications, which included a master's degree in Rural Development from the University of Sussex, England, and a bachelor's degree in Anthropology from Trinity University in Texas.

"That's correct," Naysa interjected. "And don't forget, I also hold a BS in Nursing."

"That's impressive," Vanya said. "You've dedicated time to study the culture, history, and indigenous rights of the people of this island. You've worked with the Belizean Studies task force and authored several books that are now used nationwide in secondary schools. Correct?"

Nods of appreciation came from the audience.

"You did your homework, Vanya. I'm indeed impressed." Naysa gave her a smile.

Vanya straightened in her seat and spoke directly into the microphone. "While on break, Ms. Eituk graciously took a question from a member of the audience.

"For those not in the studio, it involved tourist dollars being diverted to a new port." She looked at Angelica. "And time ran out before Ms. Eituk could respond fully. I wonder if you might like to address it now?"

"I appreciate the opportunity." Gazing into the camera, Naysa said, "I'm certain that if there is such a new port, it'll employ hundreds of Belizeans." She held up one hand to stem the rumble of dissenting voices. "It will also include some who are not originally from our shores. I'm also mindful that with each ship that comes to port, tourist dollars follow." She paused to allow her words to sink in. "My position has been, and continues to be, seeking out ways we can protect our land so that future generations may enjoy our way of life as well as creating a safe, pleasurable experience for our more than two million a year visitors."

"When you say protect, does that mean you want to do away with cruise ships?" Heads turned in multiple directions in search of the source of the inquiry. No one immediately claimed ownership of the question.

"Not at all," Naysa countered. "It's possible to protect the land and our way of life."

She watched as Ian glanced over his shoulder when her assistant, Amara Robinson, abruptly stood and stormed out of the studio, all while texting. Her flawless caramel skin was flushed, a sure sign of worry.

Just then, a middle-aged man jumped to his feet. His unusual appearance—blonde hair and drab clothing—made his sea of tattoos even more visible.

The cameraman spun in his direction.

Vanya nearly fell from her seat as she grabbed her wire-rimmed glasses for a closer examination. Her hands shot to her mouth, mimicking a child praying. "Mr. Mattison?"

Jake Mattison, an influential figure on the island, was reputed to own property near Ambergris Caye and was previously head of the KKK.

He chuckled, then snickered. "I get that a lot. The name's Preston Moscow. I work at Mattison Exclusive Resort and Spa in San Pedro. But neither my place of employment nor my brilliant boss is what I came here to discuss."

Vanya glanced at John, who wore a questioning expression. He couldn't decide whether to leave or remain and allow Moscow to speak.

"I've heard rumors regarding individuals who are seeking to hinder our citizens from earning a decent wage by stopping all ships from entering our ports."

Naysa's second superpower was what was called a resting bitch face. She mastered the look like an Olympian. Vanya, on the other hand, was an open book.

"Wait, what're you saying?" She tapped several times on the earpiece and jerked her head from side to side. "Is there someone in particular who has the power to do such a thing?"

A Black male one row back stood and balled his fists, and the female next to him placed a firm hand on his wrist. "Not here. He's not worth it."

Several others shifted in their seats and murmured their discontent.

Vanya shot from her seat, practically screaming, "Who're you talking about?"

"Her!" Preston thrust four fingers in Naysa's direction. "She claims that all ships are ruining the ecosystem and she wants to permanently shut down all ports."

Ian took several long strides and positioned himself within an arm's reach of Preston.

Rubbing her temples as though a headache was coming on, Vanya plopped down. "How could one person claim to have that much power without a position in government?"

Her eyes narrowed, and her chin tilted forward as she studied Naysa, who wondered if she'd been setup. Giving adequate time for the chatter to subside, she spoke with the confidence of someone thirty years her senior. "I do not wish to stop tourism—"

"Bull shit!" When Preston stood, the chair flipped backward, slamming into the knees of an elderly man. He started toward the stage shaking his fist. The camera panned in their direction when Ian tackled him to the floor.

A female with a pierced nose and long purple hair rose to her feet. "Mr. Moscow," she yelled. "We have to do something to protect our environment. If we don't, there will be nothing to leave for the generations to come."

"Stap yuh rass." Sweat poured down Moscow's forehead as he used local swearwords to tell the woman to shut up. His face reddened as he struggled to escape from Ian's grip. "Do you know how much money cruise liners bring to our shores? I don't give a rat's ass about the coral reef or anything else growing under—" Ian subdued him with a chokehold, silencing him instantly.

"Now who's talking shit?" Ian barked into his ear.

His second in command slapped a black zip tie around Preston's thick wrists. He yelped like a wounded dog, then screamed, "You're breaking my damn hands."

A moment later, several men in starched white shirts and blue slacks rushed into the studio.

Ian shoved Preston in the direction of an officer. "Take this piece of trash out of here."

The audience members stomped their feet while clapping their hands, chanting, "Bye-Bye," as he was ejected from the studio.

"Get your damn hands off me." Preston Moscow thrust his right elbow backward, narrowly missing a heavy-set, balding policeman's nose.

"Calm down." The officer jerked Moscow's wrists back, replacing the zip ties with steel cuffs. "Yuh mada yuh, wait mek ah beat yuh rass." His brown eyes were cold with restrained anger as he spoke through his teeth. "Make a mistake and hit me and I will make good on my promise to beat your ass."

Preston's cell flew out of his pocket in the shuffle, and Ian scooped it up. Before returning it to the officer, he looked at the screen.

Fury twisted his face, and Naysa wondered what he might have seen that made him react that way.

Her attention returned to Vanya when she said, "To say this has been a riveting show would be an understatement. "What are your plans? she continued, "Do you intend to actually stop the cruise shipping industry."

"Currently, my mission is to protect the coral reefs," Naysa said, seeking out Angelina in the audience. "I believe once the people of Belize learn what I intend to use my platform as a conservationist to do, they will join with me, use their voices, and vote for change."

"Why is this not common knowledge?" Vanya flipped her head to one side.

"Every Belizean is a stakeholder, so it's important that all parties understand my position. Once the media blitz gets underway, everything will be revealed," Naysa said, as though each word was worth gold.

"I'm so flummoxed." Vanya raked a hand through her hair, causing several strands to fall out of place. "So, what you're telling me ... us." Her hand swept out to include the audience. "Is that you believe you alone can make this change? Please explain yourself."

Eyes the color of a tropical sunset bored into Vanya's. "One thing I won't do," Naysa said in an authoritative voice, "Is justify what I've already clarified."

Chapter 3

The cell inside Sophia's back pocket vibrated. Without looking at the caller ID, she knew instantly who was on the other end, and had no plans to take his call. Besides, she couldn't answer if she wanted to. Cameras from all sides were aimed in her direction. The slightest movement would be seen by millions of viewers watching Naysa's interview.

He'd been calling for the past thirty minutes.

She expected nothing less and exhaled when the vibration finally stopped. A short chirp indicated she had a new voicemail.

With coffin-tipped manicured nails, she reached into her pocket to power off the phone. She didn't want any further interruptions while she witnessed security bounce a disgruntled attendee out the back door. She'd talk to him later.

* * *

"I don't take kindly to my calls being ignored." The man's tone was low and gravelly, but she was far from intimidated.

Sophia rolled her eyes, then removed barely visible pieces of lint from her slacks. "It wasn't intentional," she lied. Her voice defied the grimace on her face. "I was in a very public location."

"Is that so?" he asked. "The seats to the right and left of where you were sitting looked mighty empty."

"You were watching me? What the hell?" Sophia leaped to her feet and paced the perimeter of the small dressing room, where she'd locked herself in. "I've been upfront with you from day one," she said, her hand flailing in the air.

"Fu chroo?" He yelled. "When we approached you?" he snorted.

She stopped and inhaled through her nose, then exhaled slowly through her lips. With her anger arrested, calm tried to take hold. "I kept my end of the bargain. Your people have been moving throughout the islands like ghosts. Until one of your loud-mouthed associates started bragging about getting the inside scoop."

The echo of slow and deliberate hand clapping sent a chill down her spine. "Wahnti wahnti kyah get an geti geti nuh wahnti." His thick Latino accent bled through the intense words that signified he meant every word.

"Enough of that Pig Latin shit," she barked while turning the words over in her head. You always want what you can't have.

"You know damn well, that ain't no swine anything. Have you forgotten your roots?"

"Many may see you as a common horse," her father would frequently say. "But you must never forget. You are a unicorn."

Some were born with silver spoons in their mouths, she was born with a silver bullet. Revenge was her middle name. Especially until life dealt her a crushing blow. Silence choked her, but she shattered its shackles and reclaimed her voice. Like a heat-seeking missile, she'd set out to destroy her target.

Hope was for suckers. Plotting, planning, and scheming created leaders. "Enough of this pissing contest," she said, slamming her fist against the wall. "My deadline trumps yours."

"What do you need us to do?" Kennedy Kowalsky asked, exhaling loudly.

An ambulance blared in the background. "The items have been

scheduled to be delivered as you've instructed," he said, clicking the seatbelt. "Just make sure you know what the hell you're doing. My partner won't take kindly to you messing this up, so get it right."

"Or what, tilly head?" She tipped her chin in the air and laughed until she coughed.

"Who're you calling a dick head?" His question sounded like one long word.

"Oh, so now you don't like Kriol?" Sophia retrieved the M5 from the ankle holster, leaving her backup weapon in place. "It would be wise to know the players before you begin to flex." She lined the hydrostatic bullets along the edge of the marble table. A practice she'd maintained for years. It was her way of connecting to the source that ensured her enemies ceased from being a threat. "For your information, from the time I was in diapers, I snatched what was mine."

"That was your first mistake," he said, to the sound of a souped-up engine. She'd bet it was the Audi R8 he drove. "You wore diapers."

* * *

Ian lowered the window dividing the driver from the passengers. "Princess," he called over his shoulder.

Naysa shot him a disapproving look, while Luiza acted as if she didn't hear a word.

"What?" he said, shrugging. "The damn cat is already out of the bag. Besides, we may have a bigger problem."

Leaning forward, Naysa said, "All they know is that I plan to protect the reef." Then as if his statement registered, she asked, "Bigger than what?" She threw her hands up, "Bigger than the entire country learning what we fought so hard to keep hidden."

"I think the rhino in the room is that someone screwed up. How could we not know who'd be in the audience," Ian said as he side-eyed Amara. He was still feeling some kind of way with the timing of her departure from the studio and all the shenanigans that followed. Ian couldn't put his finger on it, but his senses usually weren't wrong. Until he could answer the question nagging at him, she'd be on his watch list.

Naysa squinted against the sun shining through the windshield. "What sort of problem?"

Ian passed the piece of paper back to them. This came from—"

"Let me guess," Luiza said. "Angelica?"

"You're correct." Ian waited for them to read what he had already seen.

Protecting the reef is a rouse. She's the Avenger.

"How would she know this?" Luiza yelled, bumping into Naysa as the car swerved into the next lane to prevent them from falling into a pothole the size of a small SUV. Water from the vase containing the black orchids that had been brought into the dressing room splashed onto her skirt.

"May I see that?" Amara asked, reaching past Luiza to pluck the strip of paper from Naysa's hands.

Ian snatched it away. "Rest assured, I'm going to find out who's behind this."

Chapter 4

"911. What's your emergency?" The voice on the other end was calm and soothing.

"Help me!" He screamed into the cell; his knuckles whitened under the force of his grip. "She's trying to kill me."

Cars whizzed by on either side. Some drivers held up their cells, recording the incident as if they had bought tickets to some low budget reality TV show.

Ralph would have been excited to have so much publicity at any other point, but this wasn't such a time. He was scared as hell, and no one, not even the smooth-talking operator, seemed to care.

"Lady," he screamed. "Did you hear me?" Windshield wiper fluid shot up into his face and inside his nose. He gagged and coughed. "Please help me. Hurry."

"Sir, what's your emergency?"

He pictured her sitting with the phone cradled on her right shoulder, filing her nails, and drinking stale coffee in a chipped mug.

"Hey buddy," a Hispanic male leaned out of the passenger window of a beat-up old Buick. "What the hell did you do?"

His body slid from side to side. His shoe flew off his foot as the phone fell from his hand and crashed to the pavement. "Please call the police," he begged.

The youth laughed, saying, "I ain't calling nobody. Whatever your ass did, most likely you deserve it."

The driver joined him in a belly laugh as they slowly rolled up the window then sped off.

The metal of the hood bit into his hands. Blood mixed with the windshield washer fluid making it nearly impossible to hold on. "I ain't dying like this." He released one hand and pounded on the glass. He kept hitting despite the pain.

* * *

She hit the emergency call button with a stiletto-tipped, manicured finger.

"911. Fire, rescue, or police?" He sounded as if he was reading from a script.

"Police, please." Her voice was even and calm. "You sound new?"

He chuckled into the receiver. "Is it that obvious?" he asked.

"It is. It's your lucky day. You might never get a call like this, again."

The flashing light and siren ended the conversation. "Well, I guess you'll have to find out from the news report. The police have just pulled up."

She hit the disconnect button, signaled she was pulling over, and coasted to the shoulder on the highway.

Before the vehicle stopped, Ralph Presley jumped off the hood of the vehicle and started running for the overpass.

"Stop him," Naysa screamed, jumped out of the car, and started running. "He tried to attack me."

Two officers leaped from the cruiser in hot pursuit. One ran towards Ralph, the other after Naysa. Both were tackled to the ground at the same time.

"Get off me," she screamed. "He tried to rape me."

Nails became weapons as she aimed for the officer's face. "I said get off of me." With one quick movement, he flipped her over to her belly and cuffed her.

"Calm down," he ordered. "What's your name?"

Still struggling to remove herself from his grip, she finally answered, "Naysa Eituk. Now take these things off me."

"Be still," he seethed, pushing his knee further into her lower back. "I don't want to hurt you."

The officers walked them back towards the cruiser. As soon as she was close enough to Ralph, she got in a solid kick between his legs. He went down like a sack of potatoes. Both policemen winced as if they had been kicked. The officer yanked her by the cuffs, "You really have quite the temper."

Naysa bit down on her bottom lip as tears formed in her eyes. She jerked her head to the side, using her shoulder as tissue.

"Banks," he said to his partner. "Put him into the back of the cruiser, and I'll hold this one until backup comes." He marched her to the front bumper of the police car as Ralph was shoved into the backseat. "You wanna tell me why you're driving like a maniac down the interstate," he said. "With a man on the hood of your car?"

She felt heat rise in her face and her eyes stung as her vision tunneled. "I was walking back to my car from studying in the library ..." she paused to read the nametag. "Officer Richardson. As soon as I hit the key fob to open my door, that punk came up from behind me." She shot a look through the windshield towards the backseat.

"Then what happened?" Richardson had a small notebook in his hand and a Skillcraft pen.

"He held a knife to my throat and slid his hands up my thighs." Her chest rose and fell as she spoke. "He breathed heavily in my ear and started grinding up against me."

He kept writing as she spoke. Looking up only when she stopped.

"He turned me around and tried to kiss me, and that's when I kneed him in his sack." She lunged towards the car, "Your dick is the size of my thumb, you asshole. No wonder you have to take it by force."

The officer placed a firm hand on her shoulder. "I understand you're angry, but I need you to not do that." He did little to hide his smirk. "So, how'd he end up on the hood of your car?"

Several automobiles slowed as they passed. Looky-loos broke their necks as they drove by. A school bus filled with children swerved to prevent hitting a pickup that had veered to the right trying to get a closer look.

"I got behind the wheel while he was groaning, and I tried to drive over his ass, that's how."

"You crazy bitch," Ralph yelled out of the window. "She tried to kill me. Ain't you going to arrest her?"

A second police car kicked up loose gravel as it rolled to a stop in the shoulder lane, and Richardson gently placed Naysa in the backseat. "She says he tried to attack her. He's saying she tried to kill him. Take her downtown until we can sort through this," he said to the driver.

* * *

Back at the station, Detective Ian Richardson ran her prints. He walked into the interrogation room holding a slip of paper. Pulling up a chair across from her, Ian said, "You're not under arrest. He confessed to everything, including several unsolved attacks. He's in central booking as we speak."

The chair scraped against the worn, chipped tile. "Then this means I'm free to go?"

Richardson laced his fingers and rested them on top of the documents. "It does. But I'd like to speak with you about another matter."

She took two seconds before easing back into the chair. "What can I help you with?" she asked, her eyes locked on the paper that was face down on the desk.

He followed her gaze and turned over the page. Without him saying a word, a tear formed in her eyes.

"So, you already know what I'm about to ask?"

He stood to fish out a crumpled box of tissues from the pile of items on a table and slid it across the table. She plucked the first one by the edge and immediately tossed it in the trashcan. Next, she pulled out a handful to wipe her face, then blow her nose.

"Do you have any hand sanitizer?"

"No."

Placing both hands on her lap, she exhaled. "What do you want to know?"

"Is the report accurate?"

"You read it. You tell me." She scowled at him.

"I'm not here to bust your chops over this. I just want to know what's really going on and if I should haul your ass into the holding cell with your little buddy in there." He thrust his thumb behind him towards the row of rooms surrounded by steel bars.

Inside one of them Ralph sweated profusely. A heavyset man with a torn plaid shirt and heavily soiled oversized pants inched towards him. He adjusted the slacks, folding the waistband several times. For every inch Ralph moved, his shadow followed.

Naysa smirked at the fear evident in his eyes. "The report is accurate," she finally said.

"How old are you?" he asked, then added, "Your real age, not some trumped up age you tell people in the streets."

"Last Tuesday, I turned eighteen," she said. "Before you ask. I've already emancipated." Naysa picked at a piece of skin dangling near her thumb. "Check your records."

He walked over to the water dispenser and yanked two cone-shaped paper cups from the container. Filling them, he said. "That's how I knew your actual age. Tell me again how is it that you were driving eighty miles an hour down the highway with a man dangling from the hood?"

She gave a weary sigh and paused for several moments. "You'll want to sit down to hear that answer. And you'll need something more substantial than H2O.

A smile came to Naysa's face as she recalled how she had first met Ian, and the conversation that followed. She hadn't expected to see him again, but since that time, he'd proven himself to be a formidable opponent to her enemies.

Naysa answered her phone and sat on the side of her bed.

"Good morning," the caller said. "This is Thunderstorm Artist with Fragmented Repair. I'd like to show you the progress of the repairs, if you have time this week to pay us a visit."

Naysa tapped the calendar icon on her phone then swiped several times to the left then right. "I am free today for a few hours."

"Wonderful. It's a snorkeling date."

Naysa selected a two-piece bathing suit from the lower drawer of the dresser. "Will I need to bring my own gear?" she asked. Opening the closet, she removed a wrap sundress from a satin padded hanger.

"Other than your swimwear and hat, we'll provide everything else," she said. "See you this afternoon."

"I'll be there around two o'clock."

She made her way to the living room, where Ian was speaking with two of the security agents and turned when she walked inside. He raised a finger and nodded in her direction. She went to the bar and poured a glass of wine as she waited.

"Good morning," he said, taking a seat next to her on the sofa. "What's going on?"

"Thunderstorm invited me to the reef. She wants to show me the work they have been doing," Naysa said. "Would you care to join me?"

A broad grin came on his face. "Fresh air, sunshine, swimsuit, and water? You don't have to ask me twice."

* * *

Ian parked the car in a vacant spot at Laughing Bird Caye National Park. Water stretched as far as the eye could see. He was reminded anew of how thankful he was to be living on an island and not land-locked.

Walking to the shore, they passed a sign indicating they were nearing a turtle nesting area. They paused to take in the breath-taking views. The vastness of the ocean enveloped him, and he watched as Naysa drew a long, deep breath.

Thunderstorm waved for them under the cabana. "Over here," she called. Her floral print one-piece swimsuit complemented her flawless caramel skin. Her smile widened as they approached.

Extending her hand, she greeted Naysa and then Ian. "Thank you for coming. I have sunscreen, water, and towels," she said, pointing to a waterproof container situated on a table. "I also have an extra GoPro camera if you'd like to capture some images while we are underwater."

Ian walked around the perimeter of the cabana, scanned the beach, then nodded to Naysa to indicate that the area was secure.

"It'll be just you and me going into the water," Naysa told her.

Thunderstorm eyed him as he stood a few feet from her. The bulge beneath his shirt made it obvious that he was more than equipped to meet any breach of security that might arise.

"I'm on duty," Ian said, then asked, "What are some of the greatest challenges you face in restoring the reefs?"

"Global warming," she said. "And storms. The one that affected the reef the most was Hurricane Iris. It hit Monkey River Town the hardest." Thunderstorm closed her eyes as if reflecting to that catastrophic event.

Both Naysa and Ian nodded acknowledgement.

"I would have bet the house and the car that Iris was a category five,"

Naysa said. "Who would've known anything less than a five could do that much damage."

Removing her shoes and wrap skirt, Thunderstorm placed the items in a neat pile. "We truthfully thought the damage was beyond repair."

Glancing around, Naysa said, "You'd never know anything that disastrous ever occurred here by what we see today."

"I have a phenomenal team," Thunderstorm said. "One person could never accomplish as much as we've done collectively."

Naysa removed her sundress and sandals and took both piles of clothing over to the table. Both women secured their hair with an elastic band. Once suited with full snorkel gear, they entered the water.

* * *

Ian was caught up in the memory of Naysa's firm buttocks that swayed seductively as she strolled down the beach. The white swim bottoms left little to the imagination and her olive skin glistened from the cocoa butter scented sunscreen. The sight of her firm breasts contained within the white and silver bikini top nearly sent him into overdrive.

He shifted his weight and adjusted his slacks for comfort. Then, he glanced around, ensuring no one witnessed what he'd just done. His desire for Naysa was mounting and he was skating on thin ice. Luiza wouldn't think twice about cutting him off at the knees if she had the slightest inkling that his intentions involved anything more than protecting Naysa. But he was willing to take that chance.

The reality of having to answer to her godfather and his army of Kings was a completely different matter.

Focusing his attention on the crystal-clear water and the fascinating sea life provided a visual reprieve … until Naysa floated on the surface of the water, bottom-side up. Her snorkeling hose bobbed on the waves as she dove and resurfaced time after time.

Ian reached for a stack of pamphlets sitting on the table and read about corals in between keeping his eyes on the women.

Belize was worth protecting, even if the very people for whom it was being saved, were at times clueless as to the importance of the work being done.

After taking a bottle of water from the cooler, he sent several texts to get an update on security at the house.

Thirty minutes later, Naysa and Thunderstorm walked onto the shore, laughing and talking loudly.

"That was absolutely spectacular," Naysa said as soon as Ian passed her a towel. "Fish, coral … the colors are nearly indescribable. I can't swear to it, but I am certain I saw at least half of the four hundred and fifty fish species."

"My team hopes to eventually do work with the protected areas of the island," Thunderstorm said.

Naysa squeezed water from her hair as she spoke. "I have knowledge of Blue Hole Natural Monument and Half Moon Caye Natural Monument," she said.

"When time permits," Thunderstorm said. "I'd like to share with you about South Water Caye Marine Reserve, Glover's Reef, and the others."

"Others?" asked Ian.

"Yes, there are seven areas in total," Thunderstorm replied.

"I'd like that." Naysa glanced in the direction of a cruise ship sailing on the horizon moving so slowly, it seemed to be standing still.

"We love that tourist come to the island," Thunderstorm said, gathering the supplies. "The danger comes from spilled oil and raw sewage. But the real damage comes from the ships themselves."

"I understand the harm from fuel and waste," Ian said. "How do the ships physically cause that?"

Thunderstorm asked if they might take a seat and motioned towards the cabana. "We can discuss more while hydrating."

She selected several bottles of fruit infused water and fresh-cut fruit from the cooler. Ian declined, but Naysa and Thunderstorm enjoyed papaya, starfruit, melon, and berries.

"Grounding and anchoring problems have been documented since the 1970s," Thunderstorm said. "They inflict severe scathe. Or injury, to the coral reefs, with their giant anchors and anchor chains."

"I imagine the harm would be extensive," Naysa said, sipping from a bottle of water.

Nodding, Thunderstorm added, "The damaged reef may never recover, and even if it does, it may take about fifty years or so."

Ian's cell vibrated, and he angled his body away from them to answer.

"I can never thank you enough, Ms. Eituk, for partnering with my organization."

"It's my pleasure," Naysa said, glancing towards Ian whose intense gaze connected with hers.

She cleaned the sand from her feet, then put on her sandals and stood. "Thank you for being my tour guide and for answering our questions about the work you're doing," Naysa said.

"Let's schedule a meeting later next week so we can iron out a few more details," Naysa said. "I'm really looking forward to doing all I can to bring awareness to the amazing work you are doing."

Naysa walked alongside Ian to the car. He was still on the phone, but when they sat in the vehicle and were belted in, he ended the call.

"A suspicious package arrived at the house," he said.

Naysa's head quickly jerked in his direction. "Is my mother safe?" she asked at a pitch that was much higher than normal and conveyed her stress and anxiety.

"Everyone is fine. She, Amara, and the staff were all moved away from the building as soon as it was discovered.

"Can't you drive any faster?" she asked, staring out the side window.

"My men are with them, there's no sense in us getting into an accident en route," he said placing his hand on top of hers. When next he glanced at her, Naysa's legs were restless.

"What have I gotten us into?" she asked as tears streamed down her face.

Chapter 6

"Ms. Eituk," Brooke, the slender assistant greeted Naysa as she entered the room. Dark wood paneling went from ceiling to floor. Rich textures and luxurious fabrics made the room look more like a cigar and bourbon room than a boardroom.

"Please have a seat," she motioned towards a pair of empty seats near the head of the table. "May I offer you water, tea, or coffee?"

Naysa and Ian declined.

"I'm Mason Cole and joining us for the meeting are Jarrett Davidson and Emily Smollett." His confidence came from more than the custom designed suit that showcased his amazing, fit physique. It came from years of sitting at the feet of three eras of economic leaders. He represented four generations of successful financial brokers residing in Belize.

Caye Memorável was located just five miles away from Amgergris Caye, a five-acre island promising to exceed the definition of its name, memorable.

"As you know," he said. "Our island is the ultimate retreat for couples seeking pampered relaxation and privacy. We are the celebrity hotspot. As such, we support your efforts in preserving our natural environment."

"I've heard amazing things about your resort," Naysa said.

"We know full well, that carbon emission is the main driver behind the rise in global temperatures." Emily said, her neatly manicured hands folded atop the large mahogany wood table. Unlike her male counterparts, she wore a simple cobalt dress with an a-symmetric cutout over one shoulder. The shade of blue made the grey of her eyes appear translucent. Emily's blond hair was pulled neatly back into a loose bun.

"Which in turn causes an increase in hurricanes, the rise in sea levels, and the flooding, fires, and devastation that we have seen worldwide," she said. "Cruise ships add to this by producing toxic wastewater."

Ian shifted his weight in the seat as he looked around the room.

"In respect of the coral reefs," Naysa said, "it is the focus of our partnership with Ms. Thunderstorm, Artist."

"Don't you think, Ms. Eituk," Jarrett's hazel eyes sparkled against his cream silk shirt, which emphasized his olive complexion. The fitting of his jacket and slacks were just as impressive in tailoring as Mason's. "That by drawing a line in the sand with the cruise industry, you have created an enemy where none was needed?"

"I assume your comment is in reference to the interview feature several weeks ago." Nods met her gaze, and she added, "I assure you, that was not my intention, nor is it reflective of the partnership we have with Ms. Artist and Fragmented Repair."

A collective exhale sounded throughout the room.

"The hotels obviously are not getting a benefit from cruise passengers," Jarrett said. "Even though we are the biggest taxpayers on the island. Selfishly, we have our own interest, even beyond our desire to protect the reef for future generations."

"We can prevent damage and degradation in the ways that cruises navigate shipping lanes," Mason said. "We can mandate that ships observe and adhere to regulations set in place concerning waste and pollution."

"By doing so," Emily chimed in. "We can avoid damaging the seabed and those prized coral reefs every time travelers sail upon our beautiful aquamarine waters."

"Precisely," Naysa said. "What we need most is awareness of the importance of protecting our coral reefs and your financial support for the work Thunderstorm and her team is doing."

"Is it true," Brooke asked from across the room. "That Ms. Artist singlehandedly planted all the coral to replenish the reef in the Placencia community?"

"She will tell you she had assistance, but the truth of the matter is, it all began with just her." Naysa said as she stood, and Ian followed suit. "Thank you for this meeting and for your support. I look forward to working with all of you."

"Ms. Eituk," Mason said, as they turned to leave the room. "I invite you to stay in our glass bottom suites for a get-away, or honeymoon."

His gaze shifted from Naysa to Ian.

"Thank you, Mr. Cole," she said as her face flushed. "I will keep that in mind."

Chapter 7

Hot tears streamed from Luiza's hazel eyes, though she tried to hold them in. By now, she was certain she looked as if the professional make-up artist's only mission was to transform her into a drunken racoon. Luiza could tolerate resembling a rabid procyonid but what she'd never permit was for anyone to mistake her as being weak. Even if the person responsible for the waterworks was the same man who saved her, and her then unborn child's life.

Her jawline tightened so fiercely, Luiza instantly developed a migraine. The excruciating pain was a welcome reprieve. It gave her a safe place to direct all her pent-up anger and hostility.

"Luiza, please do not cry." Khalil's legendary smile was barely visible behind the well-groomed, salt-n-pepper lush beard. The rhythmic cadence of his speech was heavy with concern. Soft chestnut eyes narrowed as he pleaded with her. "I invited you and Naysa to The Castle for a visit … and to offer a proposition, not to infuriate you."

She scanned the living area of the exquisite suite and the guards just out of earshot.

After drying her eyes, Luiza glanced at her reflection in the ornate, wall-sized mirror. Her face still had its youthful glow, but injury had taken a toll on her body. Being restricted to the wheelchair had stolen her athletic figure. Sure, she enjoyed the aquatic workouts, but she longed for the days she'd run miles on end. The sensation of the wind blowing in her hair was a thing of the past.

She slowly exhaled, and her shoulders relaxed. Luiza finally found her voice. Although shaky, it was audible. "I know," she said, then blew her nose in a tissue, her daughter, Naysa handed to her. If she was completely honest, she'd confess that she welcomed the release. A debilitating frustration had gripped her soul—she was just clueless as to which button she needed to press.

But Khalil had known.

In one short sentence, he transformed her from the badass persona she'd created over the last thirty-two years back to the world changing friend he'd always known her to be.

Khalil's footfalls were soft as he walked over to the hand-carved, ornate bar and retrieved three crystal glasses. The light from the overhead chandelier danced off the earthy colors and deep veining of the bocate wood bar top.

He dropped several ice cubes into each glass. "Would either of you care to sample a little Isabella Islay Whiskey?" he offered.

"What?" Naysa and Luiza yelled, their voices so perfectly synchronized, they sounded like one person shouting.

Placing both hands firmly on her hips, Naysa scolded him. "Papa Khalil," she said sounding more like the parent of the trio. "I know you didn't waste that much money on one bottle of liquor." Her index finger wagged as her wrist rolled with each word.

"Now that I have your attention," he said. "Can we get to the matter at hand?" He let out a deep breath.

"And for the record," he said. "You know good and well that the Castle could do a lot of good with six million dollars."

Naysa wheeled Luiza to the side of a massive, red Italian leather sofa, then took the empty seat beside her. Khalil handed them each a glass of Remi Martin cognac.

"Not quite as exotic as the other, but just as delicious," Naysa said after taking a sip.

"When I was a child, this table seemed enormous." She ran her fingers along the engravings. "Do you remember when I bumped my head on the edge?"

"Remember?" Khalil said as he sat on the hand-carved, ornate leather-and-wood chaise. "I nearly fainted when I saw the blood pouring down your tiny face."

Snapping her head in their direction, Luiza inquired, "When did this take place and why am I just learning of it?"

Naysa and Khalil pointed to each other and laughed as if to say the other was responsible.

"Good answer." A slight smile emerged on Luiza's face, then just as quickly vanished. Shifting on the cushion of the wheelchair, she asked, "Tell me more about why we're here today."

* * *

The tinge of sadness surrounding Luiza reminded Khalil of the very first day she came to The Castle. She'd just endured the most horrific event in her life. He feared what would have happened if she and the unborn baby had not survived the vicious attack. Seeing Naysa as a grown, formidable warrior, made his soul smile. A sense of peace enveloped his entire being. He couldn't have been prouder of Naysa had he been her father, and he relished being her godfather.

"The Kings have taken notice of the work you two are doing."

"I thought we were operating under the radar," Naysa's tone was cautious as she tilted her angular face in his direction. "Are they hearing of our work secondhand…and by this, I mean through a little birdie?"

A grin exploded over his face. Khalil was certain it was bright enough to eclipse the sun. "It is no secret that I'm proud of the two of you," he said. "So, perhaps, I shared with one or three Kings—by three, I mean all—the phenomenal work you're doing to help those trapped in domestic violence."

"I hear you chirping, baby bird," Luiza said, finally smiling. "What are the Kings proposing?"

"Careful, mother," Naysa warned, with a smirk. "Chicago has treacherous winters, and your sun-loving skin has become mighty fond of Caribbean weather."

Khalil cocked one brow as he quipped, "You mean, you wouldn't want to be bundled up in multiple layers from head to toe, trudging through ten feet of snow just to make your way to your automobile?"

"Not a chance," the ladies said in unison.

"Perhaps," Khalil said, cocking his head to the left. "The ability to trade in a Gibnut for a breaded steak sandwich from Ricobene's might persuade you."

Luiza's face twisted, "They may have served that rodent to Queen Elizabeth, but I am not the one."

Khalil doubled over in laughter, "Her highness is too high to dine upon the royal rat, I see."

After a slight rap at the door, and being told to enter, one of Khalil's bodyguards appeared in the entrance to the suite.

Ian Richardson, head of Naysa's security team, entered the room. He nodded hello to everyone and positioned himself a few feet behind Naysa.

Following a recent increase in threatening letters, calls, and emails to Naysa, Ian increased their security surveillance to twenty-four hours a day.

"The Kings would like to offer you both the ability to expand your mission by way of a partnership with an organization known as A Place to Ponder."

"I've not heard of them," Naysa chimed in. "What do they do and who heads up the operation?"

For approximately thirty minutes, Khalil detailed what he knew of the organization founded by two Mavericks basketball players, Adrian Hernandez and Dallas Avery. "Joining their team will require more security," Khalil said. "You will instantly go from helping a few individuals to countless numbers of women in some tricky situations."

"I'm more than capable of doing my job," Ian exclaimed as his blue eyes hardened, and his lips flattened and became virtually invisible. The black, fitted shirt threatened to burst at the seams when his muscular arms folded across an expansive chest. His smooth ivory skin flushed at the offense.

I've chosen well for Naysa.

Khalil stood and two members of his security team took a step forward. He motioned with his hand for them to stand down.

"I meant no offense," he said in a level tone. "Should Naysa and Luiza expand their efforts, the targets on their backs might grow exponentially." He eyed Ian with skepticism. "I'd think you'd welcome the best protection humanly available."

"You had enough confidence in me to assign me this detail." Ian's expression turned stubborn as his gaze slid to Naysa. "And like I said, I'm more than capable of protecting what's mine."

"That may be so," Khalil glanced at Luiza, then Naysa. "But I'm not willing to take that risk. Already, there are threats against them that warrant Marco Salazar joining you. We don't need an escalation to take preventive measures."

Marco Salazar was the Cleaner. Khalil called him out for special missions or in this case, when the client held a special place in his heart. As an ex-cop, Ian still possessed a propensity for rules and coloring within the lines. Marco wouldn't understand the definition of decorum if it bit him in the ass.

Chapter 8

"You're awfully quiet on that end," Khalil's statement broke through her moment of introspection as she stared at the horizon. "What's been going on since you've returned to Belize?"

Luiza sighed, then spoke into the headset. "That list is longer than you could imagine."

"Is there anything I need to be concerned about?"

"To be truthful, I'm not so much concerned about the work we're doing, but Naysa's safety."

She pictured Khalil giving orders to his security team and preparing them to take a quick flight to the Caribbean island. "Luiza, you're making this sound personal. I wasn't there the first time—"

She massaged the ridge of her nose, then closed her eyes. "I've been thinking about your proposition." Following several moments of silence, she added, "The need for my work to expand is more apparent than ever. But I hope I haven't waited too late to …"

"A Place to Ponder is expanding their territories."

"I think I'm ready," she said. "I know I am."

Following the attempted double murder in which Robert was killed, Luiza survived being shot by his ex-wife's father. The dark secret that she'd never shared with anyone was the catalyst that made her want to help others. Naysa shared her passion and together, the mother and daughter team became avengers of sorts. With the aid of the Kings, they'd rescued hundreds of women in difficult situations. The women received new identities, homes, jobs, therapy, and financial resources. For extreme cases, some elected to undergo plastic surgery to begin their new lives without the need to live in fear.

"Luiza," he said calmly. "Things have changed. It isn't as easy as it once was to move people around."

"Don't you dare say I'm not as young as I once was."

"I don't have to," Khalil chuckled. "You already said it for me."

They enjoyed a good laugh. "I can't just sit around doing nothing when so many people can use my help."

"Agreed, let me think about the logistics." In an unexpected change of direction, he said, "Is Naysa still leading Ian around by the nose?" he asked.

"He's smitten—"

"So, you're finally admitting he's infatuated?"

"If I could have finished my statement, you'd have heard me say, he doesn't have a snowball's chance in hell. Besides, I wouldn't swear to it, but I sense there may be a bit of competition in the house." Luiza glanced in the direction of the door.

"Isn't he a bit young for your taste?"

Luiza laughed loudly, "If that is another old-age joke, I am going to return and show you a thing or two. I think I see a spark in Amara's eye when he comes around. But Ian seems oblivious.

"My money's on Team Naysa."

"Unless Ian knows where a secret stash of gold is buried, he'd do better to dig elsewhere," she said, brushing a strand of hair off her face.

"You have to commend him for his fortitude. Hopefully, Naysa won't crush his dreams. I like the guy," he said. "Before you ask. Yes, I just sent a message to Adrian Hernandez. I've asked him to reach out to me."

Her tone was soft when she said, "Thank you."

"You truly are a hard character to get around," he mused. "My main concern is keeping you and Naysa safe."

Luiza wheeled herself to the sauna and arrived just as Naysa entered. Passing her the phone, she teased, "It's your godfather. He's particularly ornery today."

"Hello, Papa Khalil," Naysa said, dabbing her face with a plush white Egyptian bath towel. "I hope mom isn't putting you up to anything that could get her in trouble." She gave Luiza a quizzical expression.

"I'd let you know if she did," he said. "I just caught the replay of the interview. You did an amazing job."

"Thank you," Naysa said. "I haven't received an answer to my text."

"What text?" Luiza said, reaching again for the phone. She shot a questioning look at Naysa but received no further details.

"You, my friend, have gumption," he said. "The email is coming your way. Think this through before committing to anything."

"All it means is that we'll have more ground to cover."

"Which is cause for concern," Khalil said. "You'll be giving up more time and taking on much more."

"And when has that ever been a problem?"

Khalil released a soft chuckle. "That, right there is the issue. You've never backed down from a challenge, even if it puts your life in danger."

* * *

"Hello, Princess." He steadied himself against the doorframe and willed his feet to not rush to her side. He longed to touch her, taste her, tease every inch of her body. I want her, the question is does she want me, too?

Heat rose in his face, and he glanced across the room to see if Luiza noticed.

"Ian," Naysa said by way of a greeting as she stared at him, then turned and moved towards the closet.

Today, she would be on another television station being interviewed about her position on the reef as well as the work she was doing with abused women. The request had come on the same day of the interview that descended into chaos.

Again, he fixed his gaze on Naysa as the soft lights of the chandelier danced around her and reflected in her exotic copper-flecked, greenish-grey eyes.

"What did we agree upon regarding that title?" Naysa said as she planted a hand firmly on her hip. "You want to start a war where none is required."

"I agree," Luiza responded with obvious pride. "Naysa was practically born with a diamond-studded tiara."

"Enough you two, can we keep our focus on the mission. Where are we with getting signatures for the reef project?" Her mouth closed, then quickly parted as Luiza's comment registered. "And seriously, Mother. Born with a tiara?"

Laughing, "Well, it felt like you were emerging with a crown on your head. Regarding the signatures," she removed a tablet from a pocket on the side of the wheelchair. "Last count, we had just shy of seventy-two thousand signatures."

"Twenty percent of the population is not a bad start," Naysa said.

"Good morning, everyone." Amara entered the dressing room through hand-carved, ziricote double doors. Her stocking feet made a faint sound as she sashayed to the closet.

A servant had once commented about her and Naysa's similar physical features.

"Has anyone ever told you how much you and Ms. Eituk resemble? You both have the same striking almond-shaped, copper flecked eyes, high cheekbones, and prominent nose."

"If so," Amara had responded. "Then we're sisters from another mister."

"The makeup artist and hairstylists are ready for you," Amara said, holding up a dress and picking up a pair of antique emerald and ruby earrings. "These are stunning." The green color vibrant against her caramel skin and onyx tresses.

"I gave them to Naysa when she turned thirteen." Luiza held out her hand. "They were given to me—"

"During the first date with my dad." Naysa smiled broadly.

Amara placed the earrings inside her palm as if weighing them. "That's an extravagant token of love."

As he studied Amara, Ian couldn't help noticing the flash of envy—and another emotion he couldn't name—in her eyes.

His gaze shifted when Luiza grabbed and returned the heirlooms to their rightful place without another word.

Chapter 9

Luiza and Naysa settled in the sitting room adjacent to the master bedroom. The West wing alone was nearly four thousand square feet.

Naysa walked to the large window overlooking the lush English gardens. The lights looked like tiny fairies dancing in the evening sky. "I never asked, what did you think about the interview from the other day?" she glanced over her shoulder in her mother's direction.

"As always, you did a phenomenal job," Luiza said. "It was obvious there were individuals who came with their own agendas."

"Did you see Vanya's excitement when she thought Jake Mattison was in the audience?" Naysa removed her hair tie, allowing the waves to fall to her shoulders.

"Who could admire a man who wore the title of Grand Wizard? I don't care if it was for a day or twenty years." Luiza scoffed in disdain.

"He makes El Sisimito quake in his itty-bitty shoes." Naysa said, referring to mythological character who because of a thumbnail complex was believed to have gone throughout the island cutting off thumbs.

Rubbing her eyes, Luiza said, "The first time I heard about the thumbless dwarf wearing a red hat, playing a silver guitar, I laughed."

"Remember my reaction when I learned of the rumor that he cuts off people's thumbs?"

"I thought you'd never take your hands out of your pockets."

Naysa sighed then said, "I question why he's on our island."

With a quizzical expression, Luiza asked, "Who, the goblin? You know that is just a folklore."

Naysa shook her head. "No mother, not him."

"We might need to investigate this a bit further." Luiza yawned and stretched her arms above her head.

"Looks like the only thing you'll be checking right now is your eyelids for cracks." They laughed at their long-standing joke. "Come, I'll accompany you to your room." Naysa sent a text then escorted her mother to her room. When she returned, Amara was waiting for her.

* * *

Amara stood in the center of the expansive space; she was in sensory overload. Fabrics, art, scents, the sound of the waves pounding against the rocky shores as the breeze came through the open accordion doors. For anyone else, being in the presence of such beauty and not owning it would send them into a jealous rage. Not her. Envy was never her companion. Now vengeance was a bird of a different feather.

She and Naysa met in college when they were both in their freshmen year. Amara saw her signing up for an entry-level psychology class and immediately requested the course as well.

Amara's thoughts scattered when the door to the library opened.

"Thank you for meeting me," Naysa said entering the room. "Would you care for a drink?"

"A glass of red wine would be great."

Naysa pulled down two wine glasses and uncorked a bottle of La Rioja Alta Tempranillo. "Let's take a stroll while it decants."

Scents of roses, lavender, iris, and warm salt air enveloped them as they walked the path of the English-inspired garden.

"There is something magical about this place," Amara said as she plucked a floribunda rose from the branch, sniffed then placed it behind her ear.

"It's like being in a fairytale twenty-four hours a day." Inhaling deeply, Naysa placed a hand on Amara's shoulder. "I know I've said it a million times but thank you for uprooting and relocating."

"You are most welcome. There was nothing left in Texas for me …"

"You never told me what happened with your brother," Naysa said.

Amara's body stiffened, and her stride slowed. "Can we discuss Jason some other time?"

"I didn't mean to pry," Naysa said. "I would like your take on the threatening messages we've been receiving, including the letter Angelica dropped regarding our mission."

They removed their shoes to walk on the sand. "I think we need to pay attention," Amara warned. "Someone is sending a message, that much is for sure."

When Naysa nodded, she continued, "I notice the tension between you and Ian and when he gets in protective mode, no one is safe from his cross hairs, not even me."

"He has his eyes on you for sure." Amara smirked and covered her mouth with one hand. "I wonder if that's all he has brushing up against you."

Naysa nudged her friend's shoulder, then chuckled. "He is here to protect us, not—"

"Not what? How many times did we watch Whitney Houston with … what's his name?" Amara snapped her fingers several times.

"Kevin Costner."

"Him." She pointed a manicured fingertip as she nodded. "Girl, tell me you don't see the resemblance."

"You're one to talk. I see how you get all sappy-eyed when he comes into the room. Perhaps it's you who wants to play the role of Rachel Marron with a world filled with glitz, glam, adoring fans, and a hot bodyguard packing big armor."

"That was one sizzlin' bedroom scene."

"It was indeed." Naysa added, "But we're forgetting one thing?"

"And what's that?"

"Neither one of us can sing. And," Naysa said. "You know my reputation with men. Need I remind you of Melvin Reichenbach?"

Amara's body warmed all over at the mention of the name. "Melvin, who'd have known with a name like that, he'd have a thang like —"

Naysa stopped walking. "I never told you about his …"

A groundskeeper pushed a metal cart down the stone path retrieving fallen branches and debris. "Good evening," he said, tipping his grey baseball cap as they walked by.

"Good evening."

Both jerked their heads backwards when they recognized his voice. "Hello, Ian," they said in unison.

When she recovered, Amara removed the flower from her ear and stuck it behind Ian's. "Hey, you."

Ian gently swatted her hand away. The rose fell to the ground. "No time for games. We've received another threat," he said. "This one more serious than a few angry words."

Naysa's brow furrowed. "What happened?" She eyed the fallen flower and her friend.

"A box was intercepted at the gate, and it contained a fake bomb—"

"Bomb!" Naysa's pitch elevated by several octaves.

Amara didn't flinch. "How do you know it was fake?" she asked.

"Every member of my team is certified in explosives. The authenticity of it is not for discussion. What is, is that you cannot just wander off the property without letting someone know. Do you understand what I'm saying?"

Amara placed a hand on Ian's chest. "Understood."

She removed it as Ian took a step back.

When he moved away, pushing the barrow, he nodded to another man standing several feet away. Amara wondered why he felt the need to disguise himself. She watched him for a moment then headed back to the house, taking quick steps. She called over her shoulder, "Naysa, I'll take a raincheck on the wine."

Chapter 10

Naysa stood on the terrace as the wind whipped the gown's thin fabric around her legs.

Palm tree-lined walkways graced the perfectly manicured lawn leading to the white sand beach. Naysa's shoulders relaxed, and she exhaled deeply. She was confident that in a previous life, she was a mermaid. The thought of swimming topless with fin as feet resulted in a deep belly laugh.

"Naysa," Ian's voice interrupted her daydream.

She gripped the sheer material at the neckline with one hand and just above her thighs with the other, then quickly retreated inside.

"There is something enchanted about the sunrise," Ian said as he stepped onto the balcony and looked at the horizon.

Naysa situated herself on the taupe, Italian leather loveseat, cradling a hand-painted beaded pillow on her lap. "Nothing compares to it," she said, pouring a glass of fresh papaya juice.

Ian took three steps to fill the space between them and held out an envelope and a single piece of paper. When Naysa's eyes didn't register recognition, he said, "This is the envelope that came with the flowers delivered to the dressing room at the news station."

"And the paper?" she glanced at it but didn't reach for it. "Let me guess. Angelina dropped it?"

"You're correct." He opened the white envelope. "It's safe to touch."

"What's that fragrance?" Naysa asked as she leaned in a bit closer. "I cannot say that I've smelled that perfume before." She inhaled a lungful of the scent, trying to ignore Ian's pheromones that stirred her senses. "There is something familiar about the—"

"Cho!" Luiza screamed as she wheeled herself onto the terrace. "Who's wearing that vulgar raw sewage scent?"

Naysa dropped the crystal glass onto the floor. Ice and liquid flowed beneath the wheels of the chair. "Mother! You startled me. Why are you screaming? I thought you were resting."

"Does this mean anything to you, Luiza?" Ian extended his hand towards her.

"Get that away from me this instant," she shrieked. She pushed back the wheels of her chair and collided with the wall. Several pictures shook. One crashed down, and the frame shattered.

Two maids ran outside with the houseman behind them.

"I've got everything covered in here," Ian commanded. "You may return to your duties."

It wasn't a suggestion, and they retreated after glancing at the mess on the floor.

Amara stepped onto the terrace just as the last staff member vacated the hallway. "What is all that noise? Is everyone alright?" Her gaze settled on the letter, which Ian had dropped on a side table. The corner of her mouth turned upwards, and a slight chuckle escaped her lips.

The muscles along Ian's jawline flexed several times. His eyes blazed. "Did I see you smirk?"

The question came down like a guillotine.

Amara stooped and adjusted the laces of her shoes. "Are you referring to me?" she asked, placing two fingers on her ankle, which made Naysa curious. What did she have under her trousers?

"I am." He lunged closer. "I'll ask you again. Did. You. Smirk?"

Stepping between them, Naysa placed a gentle hand on Ian's forearm.

"Thank you for bringing this to my attention," she said. "We'll discuss this later in the day, when heads are a bit cooler."

He turned a searing gaze on Amara, then moved towards the door. "We're testing the originals for DNA and fingerprints."

Luiza's bangles jingled as she steadied her hands on the wheels of her chair when Ian walked by.

"I came in to tell you," Amara said to Naysa, "for the past few days, we've received dozens of calls following the news interview.

"What are the people saying?" Luiza's voice cracked as she spoke. She selected a bottle of water from the portable tray and took a long sip.

Amara reached down to pick up the fallen letter. Turning her back to everyone, she held it up to her nose and inhaled deeply. "The majority of the people are in agreement," she said, facing them. "Oddly, some side with Angelina."

"That's to be expected," Naysa said. "It doesn't bother me since I'm not in a popularity contest."

They looked up when a member of the staff stepped onto the terrace. "Ma'am, breakfast is served," she said.

Luiza glanced at her watch. "We'll be there shortly. Thank you, Lena."

"I have to go," Amara announced.

Two male staff were waiting in the doorway to the living room as she left. Pointing to the broken glass on the floor, Amara instructed. "The mess is over there."

Chapter 11

"Mother," Naysa asked as they strolled along the footpath into the gardens. "Care to tell me what's going on?"

Seagulls squawked along the shore, and waves ebbed and flowed.

"This is such a beautiful night. I don't want to spoil it with any negative talk."

"You must have forgotten whose child I am." Naysa placed a hand on her mother's shoulder. "Don't make me prove it to you."

Luiza let out a chuckle. "The fragrance on the envelope is called Heaven's Breath. I've not smelled that scent in thirty-four years."

"That's almost as old as … I am."

"I was pregnant with you the last time I was near anyone wearing that vile—" Luiza convulsed as the memory of that frightening day flooded her memory.

Naysa immediately stooped beside Luiza. "Mother," she shouted.

Ian went from walking at a discreet distance to a full-on sprint.

"Luiza, are you alright?" he asked.

Waving him off, she said, "I'm …" Luiza tried to catch her breath. The more she tried breathing normally, the faster the tears fell. She gave way to the emotions.

* * *

"I have great news to share with you," Luiza said in a hushed tone. "You're never going to believe it." She caught her reflection in the picture window; she glowed as she smoothed her dress down over her midriff.

"You know how much I like surprises," Robert said. "Does it involve handcuffs and black lace thongs?"

"Has anyone called you a brat, lately?" She moved the phone from one ear to the other as she placed her purse and coat on the hook behind the door.

"Not since breakfast. Or was that lunch?" He paused for a moment. "What's going on, babe?"

* * *

"Your father was married," Luiza said in a monotone.

Naysa could barely hear her over the wash of the waves on the shore.

"Of course, he was," Naysa said. "To you."

"No, before me. He was married to someone else."

"What are you telling me, Mother?" The sand was warm against Naysa's buttocks and thighs.

Her gaze settled on Luiza, whose eyes were as distant as the Milky Way. "I never had the opportunity to even tell him about you."

Naysa squeezed her mother's hand.

"He died in a terrible incident. A horrific crime." Luiza's breathing was labored. "Ian, please help Naysa to her feet."

"What happened, Mother?" Grains of sand stuck to her skin and the pale pink silk fabric of her slacks as she stood.

"Ian, please call for someone to escort me back to my room," Luiza said. Her eyes shone with tears as she continued, "I'll tell you at another time."

"Raul and Deepak," he said into his earpiece. "Please assist Luiza to the house."

Naysa gave her mother a kiss before she was whisked away. Once she was out of earshot, she asked Ian, "Did you know anything about this?"

"I didn't, but I'll definitely check into it." He looked over his shoulder in Luiza's direction then back at her. "She may be offended when she knows you've been digging into the past."

"I'm not certain, but I'm positive of one thing," she said, removing a spider's web from her face. "I need to know what happened. All my life, I believed my father was killed during a robbery attempt."

Two joggers ran down the walkway toward the beach, and Ian stepped between them and her.

"I have something else I need to discuss with you." He paused. "There's been an increase in the amount of hate mail and threats coming through the business center," he said.

"More than the normal psychos and whack jobs?"

"Yes. You'll notice an increase in security, per our discussion with Khalil."

"I trust you." She rubbed her hands together, then spread her fingers to allow the breeze to blow through. "What did you hear about the development of the new port?"

"Several cruise lines plan to divert ships there," he said. "They've invested loads of cash into developing the resort on the island. When the announcement hits regarding your plans to protect the reefs, several hundred workers fled and went to the other Cayes for jobs."

"That's what I'd hoped to prevent," she said. "How can we educate people to look beyond the here and now and think about their future and the future of their children?"

"Sometimes, Princess," he said. "The here and now is all that people have."

The thought of their shortsightedness depressed her. After a moment, she said, "Join me for coffee, there are a few things I'd like to discuss."

"Coffee would be great." Shooting her a glance, he added, "I can also provide more details on the threats and what we'll do in the event of an emergency."

The thought of any kind of escalation made Naysa's heart jolt. This was her home, and she wanted the best for her people. Surely, there had to be a way to reach those in opposition to her plans to preserve the reef. The wellbeing of Belize was bigger than tourism dollars and greedy investors looking for a return on their money.

***

He retrieved two cups from the cupboard and cream from the small fridge. "Has Luiza sent a message to The Castle?"

"Of course, she has. I wouldn't be surprised if she was strategizing with the Kings long before things became chaotic." She loaded coffee grounds into the espresso machine then turned it on. Steam exploded from the device. Seconds later, rich hot coffee filled their mugs.

The countertop sparkled as the overhead light reflected off the soft grey markings. The taupe leather high back chairs and white cabinets fashioned a modern touch to the space.

"By now," he said looking at his watch and chuckling. "She's seriously plotting where to hide any bodies."

"Did you know Mattison was the owner of the resort?" Naysa asked.

He fiddled with the handle of the mug and took a seat at the island in the center of the kitchen. For a few seconds, he remained silent, and she got the feeling he was distracted. Ian sipped the fragrant liquid, then said, "My team and I didn't know that."

She leaned against the counter, frowning. "What's the new mission? I can't help feeling you have one."

"I could never keep anything from you," he said. "I got a call from my children. They asked if I could come for a visit."

She poured a bit more cream into her cup, stirred it in and sat next to him. "That's a great idea, since you haven't returned home in almost a year."

"Seeing them virtually has been a huge benefit, but I miss holding them in my arms," he said.

"There's nothing to stop you from going. Khalil sent enough security to guard Fort Knox. Marco alone can hold everything in place."

Ian scowled at the mention of that name. He knew the man had a thing for Naysa. How far their relationship had gone, if there was one, remained a mystery.

"How long will you be gone?" she quickly asked.

"I was wondering …" Ian said, meeting her gaze. "If you could join me?"

Staring through the window at the downtown lights, she said, "Remember when we'd just hang out?"

A broad grin appeared on his face, and he tipped one brow. "Your favorite place?"

"Celebrity Restaurant and Bar," she said.

"Your godfather had a fit." He laughed. "What's that saying? Snitches get stitches."

"I still owe you a few cuts." She hit him on the shoulder with the side of one hand.

"I'm not the one who told Khalil," Ian said, still laughing.

She gave him a dirty look. "But you told Mom."

"That's why I did," he said. "If I hadn't, there would have been hell to pay."

"So, tell me more about what's going on in Texas."

"The children have been acting out and my mother believes things must be spiraling at home," he said. "Part of me wants to believe my ex has changed, but—"

"You can't take that chance."

"Exactly." Ian rested his face in the palm of his hands. "More importantly, I don't want to go alone."

Naysa met his gaze as he spoke, and her heart pounded against her chest. *When did my feelings shift?* All her life, she'd heard her mother warn against the dangers of love, as if Cupid's arrows were dipped in cyanide. How many relationships failed long before romance had an opportunity to bud?

It wasn't just the uniform, badge, and gun, either—though those were sexy as hell—Ian made her feel protected long before she knew his first name.

"I know this is a lot to ask," his question snapped her back to reality. "But will you go with me? I need someone near who is levelheaded so that I don't go all ape-shit crazy and do something I will regret."

"Absolutely," she said, holding his hand. "I will have Amara reschedule the meeting with A Place to Ponder until after we return."

His relieved grin warmed her heart as he said, "I feel my blood pressure lowering just knowing you will accompany me."

Chapter 12

Naysa was headed for the shower when the theme song to the Jeffersons rang out. Luiza thought the tone was silly, but it reminded Naysa of the power of resiliency and of moving on up. She grabbed her purse from the side of the bed and answered it before the third ring.

The voice of a stranger greeted Naysa. "My name is Susan Pierce. A friend gave me this number."

She sounded like someone in her late twenties and had a strong Cajun accent. She shushed a crying baby, then quietly blew her nose.

"I ain't got no family or friends here in N'awlins. And I ain't got much money …"

"Susan, are you in a safe location at this moment?" Naysa asked, typing into her tablet.

"My husband is gone now," she said, sniffling. "But only for a little while. This time, it's bad, really bad. I think he broke my nose and a few ribs." Susan began crying.

Naysa pounded her fist into the mattress, and said, "How can I help you right now?"

Susan blew her nose again, "I want to get away. I can't live like this.

It's not safe for my baby or me."

"What's the address?" Naysa asked. "I have several teams in New Orleans, and one can be there shortly. I'll remain on the line as you gather a few important items."

"I already packed some clothes, my identification, and a few items for the baby," she said. "I have an aunt in Texas."

"Wonderful, Susan," she said. "Your address, please."

"It's 9872 Jeanette Street. How long before someone comes?" Fear laced her words and cracked her voice. "Umm … umm … he's going to be angry that I left ... Oh, God."

"Susan, listen to me." Naysa scanned the screen of the device in her hand that kept her updated and her words even. "Take a deep breath. I know this isn't an easy thing. You said you wanted to protect yourself and your baby, correct?"

"Umm-hmm."

"My team can get you to a safe house, and someone will instruct you from there, okay?"

"Yes, ma'am."

"Be certain to grab all debit cards, and any cash you might have." Naysa checked the time and glanced at the outfit tossed across the foot of the mattress. "Don't worry about a lot of clothing and things of that nature. Those may always be replaced."

"I have a small suitcase and backpack ready. How long before they'll be here? I need to nurse my baby." The infant's piercing cry interrupted her explanation. "It's okay, son. Mommy's here."

"I'll stay on the line with you," Naysa said as the infant's wails subsided. "What's your baby's name?"

"Richard Lewis, Jr., after his father. I call him Deuce."

"My team is less than three minutes away. Give them your cell, and they'll give you a new one in its place."

"Yes, Ma'am." Her voice trembled as she spoke. "What if Ricky comes back before they get here?"

"Don't panic," she said. "My people can handle all situations. Look outside your front window. Do you see a black Escalade parked on the street?"

Seconds later Susan answered. "Yes."

"Open the door."

While she did, Naysa sent further instructions to Max's partner, who was still in the SUV. Max, a tall, Black female with a short blonde afro would inspire confidence. Her athletic build suggested she was a powerlifter or boxer. The small, diamond chip earrings she wore in her ears and nose gave her a bad-ass vibe. In the background, Naysa heard her soothing contralto.

"Hello, Susan and little Deuce. My name is Maximum."

"She's going to take you to a safe location," Naysa said into the phone. "I'm glad you called me. Take care of yourself and Deuce."

Naysa disconnected the call and typed a few more messages before locking the tablet and securing the phone inside her purse. Then she headed into the bathroom. Once under the full force of the hot shower, and the tension seeped from her body as she inhaled a blend of exotic fruit and flowers. She washed her hair, then applied a generous amount of conditioner. While shaving, she belted out the lyrics to Alicia Keys, If I Ain't Got You.

Ian was making her think about romance, which she'd given a break since her last failed attempt. Susan's call made her suddenly grateful for a man, who was obviously a caring soul, aside from the essential role he played in her life.

Chapter 13

"Good morning, beautiful." Ian kissed Naysa and nuzzled her neck as she opened her eyes. "My thought was to bring you breakfast in bed, but I thought you'd appreciate something better."

Shifting her weight to her side, she propped an elbow onto a pillow then asked, "And what could be better than breakfast in bed?"

"I love when you smile, your nose crinkles," he said, planting a soft kiss in that area. "I thought this would be better." He leaned over to the side of the bed, retrieved a silver platter with strawberries, whipped cream, two glasses, and a chilled bottle of Dom Pérignon.

Pointing to each item individually, she said, "E-ne me-ne mi-ne moe … I think I'll start with this one." With the speed of a magician, she dipped her manicured finger into the whipped cream and smeared a healthy portion onto his cheek. Before he could open his mouth, her lips were on his face, kissing away the sweet, creamy confection.

A soft moan escaped his lips. "That was nice. My turn." Using three fingers, he heaped the cream then covered both nipples. Starting at the location of his first kiss, he slowly made a trail of love bites down her neck, across her chest, then taking his time, sucking each breast.

Naysa's head drooped backward, and her lips parted as the sounds of ecstasy escaped. When his fingers slid between her thighs and he gently stimulated her pearl, Naysa's moans grew louder.

He kissed her, moving his head back and forth as their tongues swirled together. As her stomach quaked in reaction, Ian thrust his tongue deeper, using his fingers to toy with her at the same time.

She drew her nails down his back, causing him to flex towards her.

Naysa retrieved a large strawberry from the crystal plate, took a bite, and dangled it in front of his lips for him to sample, then quickly pulled it back as the juices dripped onto her stomach. "Don't taste it there," she said, watching his eyes follow a trail from her lips to her navel and below.

He parted her thighs and followed the path of sweet juices as the fruit traveled down between her fingers. Each drop of nectar, he kissed away. He stopped to inhale her essence.

Naysa wrapped her legs around his neck, resting her heels on his shoulders. He gripped her ankles, holding them in place as he tasted her, then went in deeper. Her body rocked with each thrust of his tongue as he brought her to the brink of pleasure, over and over but never allowed her to achieve orgasmic victory.

She tried desperately to hold him in place with the strength of her legs, but he won out. Putting his weight on his knees, he lifted her buttocks and gently settled within her warmth. Like a warrior returning home, he claimed his prize. She was raptured in desire and lost in the intensity of his expression as he pleasured her.

The control he exhibited over his body while they were joined as one, was intoxicating.

"My turn," she said with a raspy voice. "We won't be needing this." She tossed the partially eaten fruit onto the tray, shifting it.

He caught the bottle of champagne just as it was about to topple to the floor.

"Luckily, this isn't open," he said.

"But I am." She chuckled, then added in a throaty voice, "To you."

Naysa enjoyed every inch of him during what was now their third round in the bedroom suite since last night.

After dinner last night, he had escorted Naysa to her room and in saying goodnight, one accidental contact stole her breath. When she looked into his eyes, the desire in them hypnotized her. Ian had closed the gap between them and whispered, "May I?" against her lips.

A slight nod increased their contact and seconds later she felt the coolness of the wall along her back and his warmth against her chest. Her arms and legs wrapped around his muscular physique, and he carried her inside the suite. Item by item, clothes were removed and under the rain head shower, two bodies became one—physically and emotionally.

Though their lovemaking was protected, each time she was connected to Ian, her emotions were fully exposed. She was free falling and loved every moment of it with this man who called the passion hidden inside her to the surface with his willingness to pleasure her in every way.

Her moans became pants, then screams of ecstasy. Release came in wave after wave, and sweet nectar flowed onto the Egyptian cotton sheets.

With a move that made her dizzy, Ian flipped her onto her belly then softly kissed down her spine, sending shivers throughout her body.

Placing his hands firmly on her hips, he brought her up onto her knees. Situating himself between her thighs while encased in her folds, he rocked back and forth. Naysa bit down hard on the pillow, snatching a handful of the sheets and duvet. She released the pillow only long enough to scream his name.

"I love the way you say my name," he panted and released her for a moment. "I want to look into your eyes."

She straddled him, her arms and legs holding him tight. Together, they swayed in rhythm to an exotic, sensual, romantic dance. Their final climax was as intense as the first one they had shared.

Chapter 14

Sophia disconnected the call after several unsuccessful attempts, then sent a two-word text, call me. Thirty seconds later, her phone rang. She punched the speaker button without saying a word.

"Ackk, ackk." He snorted, then blew his nose.

"You really need to do something about your sinuses," she said. "That sounds disgusting."

He theatrically hacked again. "I didn't know you moonlighted as a nurse."

"Keep talking, smart ass."

"What was so urgent?" he asked.

"Naysa received a visitor," she said, glancing at the painting above the fireplace. The bronze plate read Pen Cayetano Studio Gallery. She visually traced the outline of the faces of the art depicting Garifuna culture. The people of the same name were a combination of Africans and indigenous Arawaks from St. Vincent. They had been exiled to Honduras and eventually made their way to Belize. The simplicity of the bold blue, red, white, and green palette spoke to her.

"And …?" he spewed in a sarcastic manner. "Certainly, hundreds of visitors traipse through there."

"Not one that comes with evidence." She let that sink in.

"Evidence of what?"

I bet that got your attention. "Of your sloppiness. I'm not certain how long it'll be before things lead back to you, but just so you know," she warned. "They're coming your way."

"If I go down," he barked. "You'll surely go with me."

"That's where you made your first mistake," she retorted. "I'm already in hell. My goal is to bring everyone with me."

Without waiting for a response, she hurled the phone across the room. The cell slammed against the bedroom door and crashed to the floor.

* * *

"Amara," Luiza said, as she rapped the door. "Is everything okay?"

The door opened, but only a sliver of Amara's face was visible. "Everything is fine. I dropped my darn phone."

Luiza craned her neck to look through the crack to see a shattered cell on the floor. "It looks more like you smashed it."

"Butterfingers," she said, opening the door then holding both hands palm out.

"Ian called a meeting in the study," Luiza said. "You should join us, you're practically family."

Practically? Amara frowned as if she'd smelled something rotten. "Let me think about it." She slammed the door before Luiza could respond.

"Something is definitely off with that young lady," Luiza said as she wheeled herself towards the study. "Nothing a phone call can't cure."

"It's just the two of us, so far," Luiza told Ian when they met in the study. "The temperamental one will be joining at her convenience."

He removed his jacket, loosened his tie, and folded his shirt sleeves to the elbow. To Luiza, he looked like a husband returning home from a long day in the office.

"We have a situation," he said, settling in one of the Queen Anne chairs in front of the writing desk. "One that requires we alter our schedules just a bit."

"Go on," she instructed.

"Since Naysa announced she'll be working with Thunderstorm to restore the reefs …"

Narrowing her eyes, Luiza asked, "Has someone threatened my daughter?"

"Strange things have been happening over the past few weeks," he said. "Unknown individuals have tampered with the cameras, too."

Her head cocked to one side. "Who could have done that?"

Ian removed a stack of papers from a large yellow envelope. "We're looking into everyone who has joined the staff over the past few months."

"How much closer can you look? You already know what many of them wore home from the hospital the day they were born." Despite her choice of words, Luiza was not joking. "Do I need to—"

Ian removed his tie and unbuttoned several buttons of the shirt. "I've got it under control."

"Start from the beginning," Luiza said, placing both palms on her non-responsive legs.

Ian shared information relayed to him during Thunderstorm's visit the previous week. She informed him that the volunteers were being harassed with strange phone calls all hours of the night. Two workers were run off the road. The most alarming details were the suspicious packages and a letter containing a mysterious white powder that was mailed directly to Thunderstorm at her home. The police were investigating. After looking closer at the surveillance videos. "There are glitches in the film that suggest—"

"That indicate what?" Amara entered the room, yawning.

Ian cut his eyes her way.

"Nice of you to join us," Luiza said, her comment dripping with sarcasm. She then, reluctantly updated her on the information Ian shared.

"If things are getting out of hand …" Amara said, as if oblivious to the slight. "Then maybe we should have a girls' weekend at the cabin."

Shaking her head, Luiza said, "Not when our safety is in jeopardy."

Ian approached her and placed a hand on her shoulder. "It's not a bad idea. At least, we'll be in a place where we have more control over the environment."

Luiza's head went back and forth between them as if she were watching a tennis match. "Are you both insane?"

"I'll let you two discuss logistics," Amara said as she stood to leave. "I stay packed to go."

Within seconds, she was out of the room.

"Have you checked that one out?" Luiza asked. "She has issues."

"Naysa is attached to her," Ian said, scratching his head. "I will order a closer examination. Now, about getting away …"

"Where is Naysa, anyway?"

Shifting his gaze, Ian said, "She wanted to sleep in."

Eyes narrowed, Luiza stared at him. Something had changed, and she couldn't wait to get the details from Naysa.

Chapter 15

Naysa woke late in the afternoon to two empty bottles of champagne and a dozen or so partially eaten berries strewn on the duvet. She stretched both arms above her head as a bright smile blossomed on her face.

How did a brush of his hand on hers land them between her sheets? Who was she fooling? This romance had been brewing since the moment he placed her in handcuffs seventeen years ago. Her body tingled at the mere thought of being restrained.

When she first met him in Texas, she had disliked him. Now, she was grateful Khalil had brought him back into her sphere. He was what society called the strong, silent type, except when it came to the bedroom.

"Get your horny ass in the shower," she said, kicking off the covers.

She opened the glass doors, then stepped under the jets of the dual-head shower.

"I thought you were going to rest," Ian said, poking his head into the shower.

"I can't sleep the entire day away." Naysa covered her body in rich lather.

"See what powers you have over me?" he looked down to his pants.

"Join me," she said.

Amusement lit his eyes as he chuckled. "Now what kind of bodyguard would I be if I allowed you to tempt me with your feminine wiles?"

The affection in his gaze made her heart race as she thought about where their newfound connection might lead them.

* * *

After twenty minutes, Naysa returned to the bedroom with a towel wrapped around her body and hair. "I won't be long," she said. "Any special plans for the afternoon?" She selected a pair of jeans and white linen top, and lace underwear.

His eyes shone as he watched with amusement from a loveseat in the corner.

"What's so comical?" she asked, watching his reflection in the full-length mirror.

"Oh, nothing," he said. "I like the way you move."

"Then you would marvel at me on the dance floor." She snapped her fingers while moving her hands and feet in tandem. Her hips swayed from left to right.

He joined her for an impromptu dance. "Your rhythm out of bed is almost as good as between the sheets."

While nuzzling against his neck, she whispered, "You aren't so bad, either."

Naysa shooed him back to the seat while she tended to her face. When her makeup was complete, she returned the outfit to the closet and opted for a yellow cotton sundress instead.

"How did the meeting go?"

"Amara suggested a girls' get-away to the cabin," he said. "Luiza disagreed."

"What do you think?" she asked, focusing her attention on him.

Glancing around the room, then meeting her gaze, he said, "I think protecting three women in a cabin is a less daunting task than in a twenty-thousand square-foot mansion."

"When do we leave?" she asked, arching one brow.

"As soon as we return from Texas."

Chapter 16

Most other women he'd been intimately involved with needed to be rescued. Not Naysa. Ian threw her an admiring glance as they strode side by side through the Philip S.W. Goldson International Airport.

He found himself fighting to create space to occupy in her world. After their initial encounter at the university in Texas, he all but thought she was out of his life. Until he received that fateful phone call from Khalil Germaine. He was putting together a security team to protect his goddaughter and her mother. The only catch? He had to relocate to Belize. He considered living on a tropical island a win-win, especially after his failed marriage. A new environment would give him space to clear his head and what-not.

He felt like he'd won the mega lotto when he discovered that he'd be protecting Naysa.

If he expected she'd immediately jump into his waiting arms, singing, "My hero," he was in for a big surprise. Getting close to her heart proved to be the challenge of a lifetime.

Between her hectic schedule, and over-protective mother, her best friend and secretary blocked every romantic attempt. There were times when he would swear Amara was making low-key moves on him, but she'd never been explicit.

He never mentioned this to Naysa because she loved Amara and he couldn't be certain on which side of the belief coin he'd fall. The thing that made him good at his job was his talent for defusing dangerous situations. Without thinking twice about it, he sensed Amara had the propensity to be scandalous and that gave her the quality of a ticking time bomb.

They moved through a crowd going in the opposite direction, then he said, "My family is looking forward to meeting you."

Naysa glanced his way, eyes wide as if he'd taken her back. "Really?"

He dipped his head once. "They are."

"I'm a bit nervous," Naysa said, wheeling her grey carry-on to a stop.

He placed a hand around her small waist and got them moving again. "No need to be."

"What if Aria and Liam don't like me?" she said, in reference to his children. "Or if your mother thinks I'm fass."

He grinned at her use of the Kreyol term, which meant someone with loose morals.

"You're going to have fun." He joined their hands as they walked. "And who uses the word fass these days?"

They shared laughter, then Naysa said, "It was nice of your mother to invite me to come during our time in Texas."

"She is amazing. She and Dad have a special bond." A squealing toddler ran between them, followed by her mother, who grabbed hold of the child's hand.

Ian drew closer to Naysa and put a hand on her shoulder. "As I was saying, my father proposed during their second date. By their third, they were signing for a house together. All my life he'd say, 'Son, you'll know when it's right.'"

He stopped suddenly, frowning. "I guess that was the problem with my first marriage. I tried to force what I saw in my parents. I didn't get that sudden rush. That overwhelming feeling of being …" He looked at Naysa as if seeing her for the very first time. "Of being complete."

Naysa glanced away from his intense gaze.

"My mother sensed it," he said. "She saw how challenging things were with Vivian, especially following the divorce. She used the children as pawns."

"I don't want to be the reason you cannot see your children." A tear formed in the corner of her eyes, and she stopped and pressed a hand to his cheek. "I'd rather stay here than to cause trouble."

Ian brushed the tear away and cupped his hand over hers. "Our issues started years before our separation. Vivian's temper would flair up, here, or there, but I always made concessions. 'She was tired or having a bad day.' You know, stuff like that."

A girls' volleyball team surged around them. Their makeup, hair, and outfits matched perfectly.

"When did things reach a boiling point?" Naysa asked, once the giddy group left.

Her question surprised Ian. It seemed that she'd purposefully stayed clear of any conversation directly related to his ex-wife. He motioned for her to take a seat near a window overlooking the runway.

Rubbing his forehead several times, he said, "There were signs that things were not as they should be."

He planted his focus on the American rapper who entered his line of sight surrounded by security agents. "But the day the red flags started seriously waving was when she became physically abusive."

"I hope the children didn't witness this behavior," Naysa said. "That's horrible."

A mother with two children in tow walked by hurrying toward the baggage carousel. "Aria used to wear her hair in two puffs like that," he said in a reflective way, then closed his eyes and allowed a memory to fill his mental space.

"Daddy's home."

Eardrum piercing squeals filled the home with a measure of love that only the adoration of children can create. Of all that Ian had done in his life, producing two entire human beings was, hands down, his most phenomenal achievement.

"Hello, Daddy's girl." He dropped his briefcase, jacket, and lunchbox onto the floor then lifted Aria. With one swoop, he swung her squirming body over his head. Her giggles were music to his ears. Ian wished he could bottle it up and store it in a safe to remind him of these precious moments for the rest of his life.

"Not too fast, Daddy," Aria sang. "You gone make me fro up." She brought both of her tiny hands up to her mouth and clasped them tightly around her lips. He laughed so hard, he doubled over, nearly toppling Aria over to the floor. He loved his daughter and son with everything in him.

"Our life wasn't always unpleasant," he said as several airline staff strode by happily chatting about their next destination. The sound of heels clicking against marble floors coupled with the repetitious cadence of wheels on their luggage echoed their excitement.

"At one time, our home was filled with laughter and smiles. Something changed after the children were born. I scheduled appointments for her to talk with someone," he said. "I worried it was post-partum depression. She agreed to go, and things got better, for a while."

The overhead speaker shrilled as the flamboyant Asian male attendant at the airline counter flipped his raven black hair from his eyes.

"Ladies and gentlemen," he said with a slight lisp. "Welcome to American Flight 1550 traveling to Dallas, Texas."

Ian and Naysa walked to the podium and stood in line behind an elderly Vietnamese man being escorted by a young Black male.

The back of Ian's neck prickled, and he scanned the area around him. From his right, Preston Moscow approached, flanked by several men who Ian assumed was a security team.

"I was wondering where you disappeared to," Preston said.

Ian immediately stepped between Naysa and him, when he didn't back up.

The woman with the two children took one look at them and waved her hands towards a security officer.

"I'm giving you only one warning," Ian said. "You might want to keep moving."

Staring at Ian, Preston's face twisted in an ugly expression and his eyes took on a knowing glint.

"I see you upgraded your security task force's duties." Ian said, then chuckled.

"I don't want no problems," Preston said as he smirked. "I just wanted to show my respect for the lady who plans to save the entire coral reef."

He chanted down the corridor, "All hail the reef savior."

The three men with him, slapped Preston on the shoulders as he turned away.

"Y'all be safe in these streets," he pivoted and walked backward as he yelled. "Things can get dangerous, real fast."

Chapter 17

Ian secured their luggage in the overhead compartment while Naysa settled into the seat near the window.

"Don't worry about Moscow," he said. "I'll get our team on the ground to deal with him and his hoodlums."

Several minutes of silence passed between them before Naysa asked, "How did the children adjust to staying with your parents once you came to Belize?"

"They were excited at first especially with Vivian and my parents living in the same school district." As other passengers made their way to seats, he added, "They want to visit during the summer."

Naysa twirled the ring on her thumb as if she had something on her mind.

Ian stood to remove a small blanket from the carryon luggage. He sat and fastened the seatbelt just as the intercom system squawked.

While the pilot directed the flight attendants to prepare the plane for takeoff, he placed the blanket on Naysa's lap. "Get some rest, he said. "The flight is eight hours long."

She snuggled against his neck, inhaling the rich aroma of rum, cardamom, leather, and tuberose from his cologne. "I love the way you smell."

He chuckled as he quipped, "I bet you buy Bvlgari for all the men in your life, so we all smell the same."

She playfully punched him on the arm. "You're so bad. Thanks for the suggestion, though. It isn't a bad idea."

Naysa reached into her bag to retrieve a tablet and two pairs of earphones. She gave him one, then positioned a bud in her ear then pressed play.

Glancing down he said, "I love Nina Simone."

Within ten minutes, she was fast asleep. Ian traced the outline of her fingers. Moscow's derisive taunt made him uneasy. The moment he touched down; he'd get his people to send a message Moscow wouldn't forget. Better yet, he sent Marco a text. The thought of Marco being unleashed brought Ian a bit of amusement. That'll teach 'em.

* * *

Naysa woke to turbulence and a chirping sound. "How long was I asleep," she asked, watching passengers fasten their seatbelts. "Have you seen my phone?"

"Only a few hours." He passed the cell to her, then motioned for the flight attendant. "I asked them to keep lunch warm for you. I knew you'd be hungry."

"You're the best."

"I have a confession," he said, while the attendant delivered a plate with grilled chicken breast with orzo and lemon basil pesto.

She unwrapped her fork and turned fully in his direction. "And what might that be?"

His mouth twisted upward on one side and bit the inside of his bottom lip. "You've been rather secretive lately."

"I'm listening."

"Promise me," he asked, "you won't take matters regarding your father into your own hands?"

She licked her lips and rubbed them together several times.

Locking eyes with her, he said, "Naysa …" his tone authoritative.

"You're a tad bit late." Naysa rubbed the bridge of her nose. "I hired a private detective to check into his first wife."

"You did what?" he yelled, the vein in his forehead growing by the nanoseconds. "Please tell me you're just kidding and that you didn't go digging around?"

Several passengers turned in their direction. Across the aisle, an older male whispered to the grey-haired lady sitting next to him.

His gaze was heated but steady when he asked, "What have you found out?"

"His first wife is still living. She was released from jail just a few months ago," she said. "The trail ran cold after that."

"Probation and parole don't have information on her whereabouts?"

She took a sip of wine. "My informant is on leave. We have to wait until he returns next week."

Ian handed Naysa his cell. "Put the name and number of your investigator in my phone. And send him a text that he'll be dealing with me. Your sleuthing days are over."

She crossed her arms and pouted.

"Don't make me contact your godfather," he warned.

"Snitches get stitches."

"And guilt makes you tilt," he said. "You can threaten all you want, but when it comes to your safety, I'll leave no stone unturned."

Luiza wheeled herself into the study and answered her phone on the first ring. "Were you able to get them to safety?"

"They're all doing well." Augustin LeBlanc's Creole accent reminded her of the folks she'd met during the summers she spent in Haiti.

"We got to them just in time," he said. "The girlfriend was spotted a few blocks away."

"And what about the children and her mother?"

He cleared his throat. "That was the tricky part. We had to separate them for the safety of the children. The grandmother seemed sketchy."

"Sketchy how?"

"Like she'd possibly call the lover and divulge where they'd been taken."

"Where did you send them?" She wheeled over to the desk to retrieve the tablet.

"Liana Cadogan agreed to shelter them."

"London will be a good place to start over." She tapped a few keys and closed the cover. "Agustin, how many more safehouses do we have in that region?" Luiza asked.

"I'll get the exact figures to you. We have another problem," he said. "We've been experiencing attacks on our frontline workers."

"Naysa reported the issue to the Castle. The Kings are working on it," she said. "Mwen pral pale ak ou pita."

"I'll talk with you later, too," Augustin said, translating the Kriol phrase in response. "Be safe."

Luiza left the West Wing of the residence to join Amara for breakfast. Since Naysa and Ian left for Texas, she promised herself to be a bit kinder to her, but something about the woman bothered her.

"Good morning, Ms. Luiza," the butler said as Luiza positioned herself at the breakfast table. His suit fit as nicely as it had the first day she'd met him. His face still reflected genuine delight in seeing her. Except for patches of grey hair to his head and beard, he looked the same.

Xavier poured coffee into a small porcelain cup. It clinked as it tapped against the matching saucer. He lifted the silver plate cover to reveal Fry Jacks, scrambled eggs, Mayan spinach, and sauteed Chaya. In a small bowl was a healthy portion of refried beans with onions, garlic, and coconut oil. A bottle of Marie Sharp's hot sauce and a bowl of pico de gallo filled the remaining space on the plate.

"That looks delicious," Marco said, as he walked into the room. He'd been left behind to continue his job as one of six other guards around the mansion.

"How're you feeling this morning?" he asked Luiza, pulling up a chair across from her. "Did you rest well?"

She poured a glass of papaya and mango juice. Some spilled onto the white linen tablecloth and Xavier rushed to her side to clean the mess.

"I slept well," she said. "I should be asking you the same question."

"If I were to be truthful—"

"You aren't going to steal Ian's line, are you?" she asked. "Next thing you'll be trying to assume ownership of his woman and position."

A sly smile curved his lips. "Maybe I want more than Amara and last time I checked, I outrank him."

Luiza locked gazes with him, staring into his eyes and letting him know she wasn't up for any of his foolishness. Idiot. You don't have the slightest chance of success and besides, Ian isn't interested in Amara. He has the hots for Naysa.

He raised both hands. "Truce," he said. "I have a few questions."

"What do you want to know?" she asked, the question void of all patience.

"Can you tell me more about Naysa's dad?"

His question immediately spun Luiza into the past.

"Mom, where's my dad?" Large eyes, wide with curiosity, looked up from a tear-streaked face. "All the other kids have fathers, but I don't. Where's my daddy?"

Luiza maneuvered the wheelchair around several stuffed animals to reach her crying daughter. "Your daddy loves you so much," she said. "He is always with you, leading, guiding, and protecting you."

"I know, but where is he?" Her mournful wails tore at Luiza's heart. "I want my daddy," she yelled.

"Your father's in heaven, Sweetheart. But don't cry. You have me."

"Then he should have taken me, too." She screamed as she stormed out of the room.

Luiza swiped away a tear that trickled down her cheek.

The small vein along her neck pulsated as her focus returned to Marco. "That's a very personal question to start the morning, don't you think?"

He changed seats to sit next to her.

Luiza leaned in the opposite direction, but he closed the gap. "How do you feel about Ian and Naysa's relationship?"

Luiza smacked both palms against the table, which spilled the juice over the rim of the tumbler. "I don't like where this is going," she said. "You were sent here to do a job. Right now, you seem to be doing everything but." She planted a steely gaze on him. "Be the best security agent you can be and perhaps I will put in a good word to Khalil for you." With a flick of her wrist, she dismissed him.

"Hey," Amara said as Marco stormed past her.

She sat in the seat he had vacated. "What has him in such a rage?"

"He got a bit too cozy," Luiza said. "He doesn't understand there are boundaries that ought not to be crossed."

Amara averted her eyes but not quickly enough for Luiza to miss her curiosity. She was too interested in Naysa's personal affairs and had secrets of her own that might affect their family and business.

Chapter 19

In another life, Amara was known as the Drama Shark. She could smell mess a mile away. Something in her guts told her she'd stumbled upon a prime opportunity to delve deep and get messy.

She rested her elbows on the table. "What was he trying to do? Cozy up to you for intel?"

Luiza squinted, but just as quickly, her expression softened. Nodding, she sipped from her glass of juice. "Something made him think he could ask personal questions."

Blood in the water. Amara leaned forward and rested her chin on her closed fist. "Personal as in who was your last date, or as in, what brand bodywash do you use?" She could barely contain the drama queen inside her doing summersaults. If this panned out, she'd change her name to Messy Amara.

"He wanted to know about Naysa's dad."

Jeronimo! "Wow, the audacity." She removed from the sideboard a porcelain plate with fresh fruit and a warm croissant. Returning to the table, she buttered the roll and added a spoonful of black currant preserves. Xavier came to her side and poured a glass of juice, then disappeared as quietly as he came.

"In all the time Naysa and I have known each other," she said between small bites. "We have spoken very little about her father. What was he like?"

Closing her eyes as if the answer could be found behind closed lids, Luiza finally spoke.

"He was the most amazing man," she said. "His very presence made me smile."

Amara couldn't help staring at Luiza as she continued her tale. "Naysa has his almond-shaped eyes and smile," she said. "Every time I look at her, I see him smiling back at me. The part I once loved, that is."

Amara weighed her words carefully as she said, "Naysa once told me that she felt her resemblance to him brought you pain."

"I could never hide anything from her," Luiza exhaled deeply. "It saddens me that she thinks I'm mad at her, but it's complicated."

"I understand," Amara said while her nails dug into her palms, drawing blood.

"He would pull the best pranks ever," Luiza continued, stifling laughter. "I never knew what trick he'd have lurking up his sleeve."

Amara wiped her hands along her jeans. The self-inflicted wounds stung as she wished she'd never asked the hag before her any questions.

"Her father would have cherished Naysa," Luiza rambled. "She would have been the apple of his eye."

Amara pushed the chair back, causing it to scrape on the wood floor. The glass of juice spilled as she grabbed the table to stand.

"Are you feeling ill?" Luiza asked, her face a mask of concern.

Too incensed to reply, Amara walked out the door without a word.

* * *

Once the mess had been cleared away, Luiza was able to focus.

What on earth possessed me to share something that precious? I must be getting soft.

Luiza's thoughts wrapped around what might have brought on this same question from two different employees. Why were they interested in Robert?

She hadn't talked openly about the man who'd been the love of her life in many years, and now, it was as if a spring had bubbled to the surface, compelling her to speak.

Despite how she felt about her personally, Naysa trusted Amara, so maybe her suspicion was unwarranted. She squared her shoulders as she took a sip of water. A moment of vulnerability had crept upon her unawares. It wouldn't happen again. Too much was at stake for her to grow careless at this stage of her life.

Chapter 20

"Is everything okay?" Ian rolled his head while stretching his legs. His vertebrae made a cracking sound.

"All is well. Just a few issues that required my immediate attention," Naysa said, placing the cell into her back pocket.

Ian rolled their suitcases toward the rental car shuttles, but she touched his arm and pointed to a seat a few feet away. "Let's sit for a moment."

She settled on the bench and Ian sat next to her.

"You know basically everything about my life, except …" She opened her bag to retrieve her tablet.

"What I haven't shared is my why."

Ian's gaze lowered and rested on the digital device in her hands.

"Every minute, twenty people are physically abused by an intimate partner." Her voice was just above a whisper. "That's in the United States alone." She rubbed her palms along her knees. "On a typical day, more than twenty thousand phone calls are placed to domestic violence hotlines."

Ian's eyes widened and his mouth opened. He immediately closed it and said nothing.

"When I was younger," she said. "Even before the car incident, I was attacked—"

He stood, rubbing the back of his neck with one hand. "Oh, my goodness. I didn't know."

"He fared worse, trust and believe." She patted the seat for him to sit again. "It let me see, though, that not everyone would have the same outcome. My attacker was no stranger," she said. "Someone who told me he loved me in one breath, turned around and tried to stop me from ever breathing again."

"This is heavy." Ian rubbed his temples as if that would make understanding the situation easier.

"And not just one time."

A female voice squawked the names of two passengers and their gate number through the public address system. Seconds later, a couple who were arguing about shopping, lugged brightly colored carryon suitcases down the corridor. Ian followed their progress.

Naysa coughed, bringing his focus back to her. "My mother and I could never do the work on our own."

"Is that why you're considering partnering with Adrien Hernandez and Dallas Avery?"

"Yes, in part," she said. "They wanted to work in tandem so that collectively we could assist more women."

Another shuttle arrived, and dozens of people exited carrying luggage, neck pillows, or were followed by cranky, sleepy children.

"We also have key figures in places all over the world for difficult cases," she said.

"What would classify a case as being severe?" he asked.

"I get calls from those connected to high-level politicians and dignitaries. The victims aren't famous. Most abusers have partners in their lives who aren't in the spotlight. They can hide the abuse in plain sight."

"Wow." Ian scratched his head. "Where does the reef fit into all of this?"

"The coral reef project is what I feel I am called to do, to leave the world, more specifically our island better than the way I found it."

She stood and held out her hand. "Helping women is the blood coursing through my veins. Advocating is who I am. But we can go over all of this later. For now, you have a family waiting on you—"

"On us," he said, sliding his arm around her waist.

"And we don't want to disappoint them by being tardy."

"As long as we circle back to this conversation," he said. "I'm concerned with anything that affects you."

"I get the feeling you're growing fond of me." Naysa wrapped her arms around his neck, and he lifted her off her feet.

A group of college students walked by, clapping.

She tapped him on the shoulder, then brushed his lips with hers. "We're making a scene," she said, then laughed.

"That was the plan." He chuckled and kissed her again.

* * *

Ian turned away from the Avis counter with the key to a Cadillac Escalade in hand and escorted Naysa to the waiting vehicle.

"This will hold all of us should we go out to sightsee a bit," he said, as he placed their luggage in the trunk of the car.

"I'm looking forward to meeting your family and seeing a bit of Dallas," she said, while fastening her seatbelt.

Before Ian could get situated behind the wheel, his cell rang, and he answered.

"Daddy," his children sang in unison. "How was the flight?"

"Everything went great. We're in the rental car now heading your way. I cannot wait to see you."

Naysa placed her hand on his thigh as he spoke, distracting him for a second.

He pictured his son and daughter as they leaned over the cell, most likely playfully shoving to be the one nearest to the phone. He loved his family deeply and could not wait to introduce them to the newest love of his life. "I have you on speaker," he said while buckling his seat belt.

"Hi, Naysa," Aria said first, followed by her brother. "Did my daddy snore all the way here?"

Naysa laughed, "I have to be honest; I'm the one who probably snored the loudest. It was a nice, relaxing flight."

"We cannot wait to finally see you," Symone, his mother, chimed in with lots of emotion in her voice.

"We'll see you guys soon. Love you." When he ended the call, he said, "My mother is quite the romantic. I sensed the waterworks were about to start, and no need in jumping ahead too soon." He smiled broadly. "She's going to give a full show as soon as she—."

A black BMW 3 Series sped up from behind them, then shot in front and slammed on the brakes.

Ian jerked the wheel to the left, then sharply to the right causing Naysa's face to smack against the window.

"Ouch." She cupped her head. "What in the world?"

The BMW sped away, and Ian pulled over to the shoulder and parked the SUV. He snatched off his seatbelt, then faced her. "Are you alright?" He gently moved her hair aside, checking her scalp for any hidden wound.

"Follow my finger," he said as he moved his index finger from side to side as he watched her pupils.

"Okay, Dr. Oz," she said. "I'm alright, really. I've hit my head harder for play. Did you get the license plate number from that BMW?"

"Unfortunately, I didn't. I was more concerned about you. Since there are no other drivers on the road, I'm not sure what that was about." He glanced to his left, then eased the vehicle into drive.

Rubbing the forming lump on her head, Naysa said, "It seemed deliberate."

"I was thinking the same thing." He glanced at her again. "Who knows. People these days are always looking for a means to an end. They could've hoped we'd hit them from the rear to have a lawsuit. You can never be too careful these days."

Chapter 21

The front door swung wide open as soon as the SUV turned into the drive. Aria and Liam emerged from the house as if they spotted Santa's sleigh.

"Daddy!" Aria launched herself at Ian, nearly toppling him backward. He twirled her around several times.

"Stop, Daddy, you gone make me fro up," she yelled.

He burst out laughing.

"I never grow tired of hearing you say that."

After releasing her, he greeted Liam.

"Hey, Dad." The boy, who was the spitting image of his mother, Vivian, extended his hand. The only resemblance to Ian was his eyes. Liam was a handsome young man.

"You've grown quite a bit since the last time I saw you. You're what? A foot taller?" Ian shook his hand and then yanked him into a full embrace. He kissed the top of Liam's head, inhaling his scent. "You look good, son. And by the smell, I can tell someone has been receiving gifts behind the old man's back."

Aria shrugged as Liam winked at Naysa.

"We don't know what you're talking about," they responded in harmony.

With Aria on his right and Liam on his left, he said, "Children, meet ... my friend, Naysa."

She extended her hand to shake theirs.

Aria immediately hugged her tightly. "Nice to finally meet you in person."

Liam hugged her as well, then reached for her suitcase which he pulled towards the front door.

Ian proudly looked on, thinking how well Naysa would fit into his family. His smile broadened as his mother and father warmly invited the love of his life into their home and hearts.

"Hello, nice to finally meet you." Malcolm, whom Ian resembled, nodded in approval of his son's choice.

"Please, take a seat. Let's have coffee and chat." Symone approached the dining room table with a platter of homemade cookies as Malcolm grabbed four cups and cookie plates and brought them to the table. Her lean, statuesque appearance reflected a healthy lifestyle of diet, exercise, and rest. Ian had filled Naysa in on the things that kept his mother occupied. Grey tresses matched her eyes and deep dimples and laugh lines appeared when she smiled.

"Tell us all about how you two met, and don't skip a beat." Symone placed both elbows on the table, sipping a cup of black coffee.

Laughter filled the space as Naysa replayed the first day she encountered Ian while speeding with a man clinging for dear life on the hood of the car.

"Did he wink at you?" Malcolm asked, reaching for a third cookie.

Symone whacked him on the hand, causing the treat to drop back onto the platter.

"I didn't wink, did I?" Ian asked, quickly snagging the cookie that had been abandoned.

"You most certainly did," Naysa said as Symone tapped the back of her hand in approval.

"It's a losing battle, son. It will always be the ladies against us,"

Malcolm said as he stood to refresh the pot of coffee. On his way back to the table, there was a loud pounding at the door. Symone left the room to answer it.

"Where is he?" A boom reverberated throughout the house. Ian assumed the intruder had slammed the front door against the wall.

"Mom," Liam shouted.

"You heard what I said. Where is ...?"

* * *

"Whoa," Malcolm took several giant steps to shield his wife. "Have you fallen and hit your head? You will not come into my house with this level of disrespect." He stood flatfooted with both hands on his hips, preventing Vivian from moving any further.

"Mommy?" Aria came up behind her mother with concern in her eyes. "Why are you here?"

She reached for her mother's hand, but Liam took several steps back and eased up the stairs.

Vivian clenched her fists while her green eyes narrowed with anger. "I was told your dad was coming and would have his lil' bi—"

"We've always loved you, Vivian. But you will not disrupt our house." Symone marched across the room to stand beside her husband.

In a swift move, Ian stepped between them. His displeasure was clear in his forceful tone.

"Vivian, let's step outside and … talk."

With his hand in the crook of her elbow, Ian escorted her toward the door she had burst open.

He glanced up the stairs, where Liam stood on one tread with his arm around Aria. When their gazes met, fear clouded Liam's eyes.

Ian wanted to swear but clenched his jaw as he propelled Vivian toward the front porch.

Chapter 22

"I heard you'd picked up some weight." Vivian's face was distorted into a grimace.

Maintaining his composure, Ian laced his words with grace. "What is it that you need, Vivian?"

"Oh, now you're interested in my needs." Her volume was slightly lower than a scream. "I hear she's closer to your age. Go figure." She snorted. "I guess I was just too much woman for you, hum? All this time, all you really desired was a run-of-the-mill common ass babysitter." She spat out each word as if it was vomit.

The neighbor from next door stepped onto his porch to stare in their direction. Forty years ago, he and his folks were the first immigrants to move into the close-knit community. "Mr. Agbayani." He waved, hoping the man would go back inside.

"Is everything all right?" After being in the United States for decades, his Filipino accent was just as thick as day one.

Ian walked closer to the steps to prevent himself from yelling. "All is well," he said. "Just a little misunderstanding. Thank you for your concern."

He watched until the elderly man returned inside his house. "Vivian, my folks live here. This isn't the time nor the place," he said between clenched teeth. "What is it that you need, or should I say want?" he asked. "For Christ's sake. It's been five years since the divorce. You got everything you wanted. I even let you have access to half of my retirement fund, when the day comes. Hell, I even offered you the house in Hawaii and the vacation property in Colorado."

"Let me?" The words left her mouth like heat-seeking missiles. "You didn't let me do anything. My lawyer raked your ass over the flaming-hot coals, and I got it all. As for the house, you thought you would leave me stranded on some damn island halfway across the world. Texas is my home, and it's where I'll stay."

"Then what do you want?" His words were now free of every shred of patience. When she failed to respond, he walked back into the house.

"Today's visit was just a warning," she yelled.

He quickly turned around and, within nanoseconds, was back in her face. "Are you threatening me?"

She closed the tiny gap between them and whispered. "Consider it a promise. A pre-wedding gift if you will."

Ian observed the hollow space in her collarbone and sunken cheekbones. She appeared much thinner than he recalled. Vivian's nails were not their usual, perfectly manicured set, and even her hair was unkept and matted.

Before he chose to comment, Vivian turned to leave. She extended her right hand and pointed her fingers at him in the fashion of a gun. "Next time, it will be real," she said.

His eyes narrowed, "Don't count your blessings too quickly," he said. "You may never get another opportunity."

Chapter 23

"How did four days pass so quickly?" Aria asked Naysa as she folded the last of her items and placed them into the suitcase. Liam stood watching them in the doorway to the guestroom.

"I've enjoyed myself," she told them both. "This was the best visit I've had in a long time."

Aria squeezed Naysa around her waist and her eyes sparkled with tears. "I wish you could stay longer."

Naysa opened her mouth to speak, but nothing came out. She cleared her throat and wiped her eyes. "I…I'm so happy to have met you both in person. Thank you for accepting me into the family."

Liam ran to her and nearly toppled her onto the bed.

"Please stay." He clung to Naysa, sniffling.

Ian walked in as Aria nudged her way into the embrace and joined her brother in holding Naysa tight. "What am I? Chopped liver?"

The children turned in his direction, "Well, I'm too big for you to pick up and turn me around until I fro up," Aria said.

"If you pick her up, then you have to do me as well," said Liam, as he used his sleeve for a handkerchief.

Ian bear-hugged his children and a soft smile claimed Naysa's lips when he blinked hard to stop himself from joining their tear-fest.

With affection shining from his eyes, he looked at Naysa over their heads. "What do you both think about coming to Belize?"

* * *

The drive back to the airport was vastly different than it was a few days prior. Naysa warmly placed her hand on Ian's leg. "This was a beautiful four-day weekend."

"I need to involve the police and have them remove the children." He spoke as though he hadn't heard her words.

Naysa listened as he processed his thoughts.

"I think I'm going to call my lawyer as soon as we land and ask if he can try and see if the court might grant temporary custody of the kids to my parents." He tapped his fingers on the steering wheel in a rapid beat. "They can remain there until we send for them to join me."

Naysa locked eyes with him for a second or two. She had no objection to him wanting his kids with him.

"I'm so sorry we landed smack dab in the middle of some serious baby-momma drama. I should have done this before we made the trip." He reached into his back pocket when Naya's phone rang.

"Mother?" the words emerged more like a question than a greeting. "Is everything okay?"

"I don't mean to interrupt your vacation—"

"Nonsense," she said, tapping the space between her eyebrows. "What's going on?"

Luiza exhaled slowly before speaking. "Thunderstorm has been found murdered in her studio." Her words barely audible as she continued, "How soon before you two return?"

Chapter 24

"I expected something …" Amara said, observing the space. "Fancier."

The decision to relocate to the cabin was made with some trepidation. Amara insisted it was what was needed to take everyone's mind off the drama while Marco and Ian contemplated the logistics required to provide adequate security. In the end, both determined locking down an eighteen hundred square foot cabin was considerably easier than their current residence. Against Ian's objections, Khalil detailed extra security.

"This is the way Naysa's dad had it built." Luiza emotions were frayed, and she didn't have the bandwidth to dial back her sarcasm. "We saw no reason to change it."

Ian, who sat at a wooden table near the back of the room, gave Amara a disapproving look but didn't comment.

Luiza took several deep breaths. "What are the police saying about the murder?"

"They are in the preliminary stages of their investigation," Ian said, "but I have a man on the ground and should soon have some information."

Naysa reached into the upper cabinet and pulled down several mugs, which she rinsed in warm water. Next, she filled a tea kettle and placed it on the small range. Reaching into a drawer next to the sink, she took out several tea bags and placed them on a saucer which sat on a tray on the counter.

"I just texted Khalil asking him to check into it as well," Luiza said.

Adding a jar of honey to the items on the tray, Naysa responded, "I'm certain he will find out something soon." She went still as tears filled her eyes. "I really liked her."

"She singlehandedly conquered a mountain and scaled it down to a manageable size."

Nodding, Luiza said, "Thunderstorm not only tamed Goliath; she made him her servant."

Naysa laid the tray on the table and met Luiza's gaze. "How one woman could have taken on the gigantic task of replacing the entire coral reef system is beyond me."

* * *

An agent tapped on the door and walked inside. His freckles, red hair, and glasses earned him the nickname of the character from the cartoon, Rugrats.

"Jarul needs you outside, Ian," he said.

Jarul Rusnick was the first agent Ian hired upon coming to work at the residence. Over time, Ian had come to trust him like a brother. Of late, Jarul had been distancing himself. Stressful situations had a way of bringing out the inner character of individuals. The climate of the residence was bringing to the forefront a multitude of personal demons.

Ian kept his gaze on Naysa, while he spoke, as if compelled to look at her. "I'll be there in a few minutes, Finster."

Luiza wheeled over to the hearth, retrieved the poker and smacked it against the logs in the fireplace. Embers flew up through the chimney. She reflected that the wood burned nearly as hot as Ian's temper after hearing the Kings would soon take over securing the residence.

Amara palmed each item throughout the cabin in a slow tour of the space. Gripping an oversized pillow, she sat on a cushioned chair. "This is very unusual fabric, where did it come from?"

"That was made from a blanket that was given to my father by his dad." Naysa stretched out her hand for the pillow.

Amara jumped to her feet, causing the chair legs to get tangled in the weave of the small rug, and it crashed to the floor. She tried to force her way past Ian, who blocked her path. "Move, I need some air."

"Let her go," Luiza said. "Maybe the fresh air will do her some good." She poured a cup of tea then wheeled her chair to the bar she had sculpted from Jobillo wood. The deep-orange veining brought the bar to life.

"Would you care to add anything to your tea?" She removed several bottles of vodka, rum, and bourbon.

Ian returned the bottles with a gentle reprimand. "We need to stay focused."

* * *

"Amara. Wait up." Jarul ran to catch up then held on to her. She yanked her arm from his grip and continued walking.

He reached for her shoulder again, and she swatted his hand away. "Don't touch me."

"Aahnti wahnti kyah geti an geti geti nuh wahnti," he said. "You always want what you can't have."

She immediately stopped and focused on him. "What did you say to—?"

"You heard me," he barked.

The harsh tone flipped a switch in her brain, and she gaped at him. "Your voice is … different." She eyed him with skepticism.

"Nothing that a hundred-dollar voice altering device couldn't provide," he said. "They're making them more realistic as time goes by."

She stood silent for a few moments. "I never liked your ass anyway. You just smelled sneaky."

If she revealed her hand now, all her plans would be shot to hell. He foolishly believed he was in contract with her to stop the replenishing of the reef. Fool. Her plans far exceeded financial gain. She was in the fight for pure, unadulterated revenge.

"All this time, it was you." She wagged a finger in his face, then lowered herself to sit on the grass. You're Kennedy?"

"I can't take all the praise. I did have a partner, but …" He smirked as he sat next to her. "I could say the same thing, Sophia."

"How did you infiltrate the security team? You must have some strong connections because every man employed here has been vetted."

"Let's just say I slid in after taking out one of their people."

"That's impossible." Amara thought for a moment then gaped. She hadn't seen one of the guards in some time. "What did you do to Audley?"

"Wouldn't you like to know."

In the distance, a Black Howler growled.

Amara stiffened, then scanned the area.

"Don't worry about the baboons," he said with a curl to his lips. "It's the scorpions, black widows, and bullet ants you should fear."

She immediately scrambled to her feet, dusted off her pants, and kept walking. Another moment to settle her brain was in order. She'd come too far now for rash action.

"What's going on inside the cabin?" Jarul aka Kennedy asked.

"Nothing that concerns you," she said.

"To the contrary." he sneered and clamped a hand around her arm. "Everything about you and them concerns me. I'll ask you again, what's going on?"

Chapter 25

"Finster, where is Jarul?" Ian asked via radio communication after ending a call on his cell.

"I don't know," the young man replied. "He ran after the secretary."

Ian peered into the darkness of the night, seeing only a few fireflies and hearing the growl of the occasional baird tapir. He spoke into his earwig, "Jarul, report back to the cabin immediately."

He deeply inhaled the night air a few times before going back inside. Something wasn't right, which left him on edge.

***

"What does he want," Amara asked, hearing Ian's voice echoing from Jarul's earpiece.

"I assume by now he's learned the bullet that killed Thunderstorm came from my backup weapon."

She stepped back and put a safe distance between them as her heart pounded. "Why did you kill her?"

Pointing to himself, "What do you mean, 'why did I?' The question you should be asking is, why did you set her up? You had to have known it wouldn't be long before we decided which of these two do-gooders is the heavier liability."

Amara's head cocked to the side, and her eyebrows winged upward. "What do you mean 'we'?"

Jarul flipped his wrist and continued talking. "We couldn't afford any distractions, seeing that we're so close to the completion of the Caye."

He walked towards the mountains. "I have invested more money into this project than you'll ever see in three lifetimes. I'm not losing a single dime."

Shaking her head, she said, "So, you killed an innocent woman?"

"You killed her the moment you brought her into your bogus game of cat and mouse."

"Jarul, return to the cabin, immediately." Ian's voice boomed through the earpiece.

He pulled out his cell and hit the redial button.

"Ian," he said. "I'm on my way back. I thought I heard something rustling in the trees, but it was only a rabbit." He ended the call, then jerked his head in her direction.

"You heard that?" he asked. "Sorry to burst your bubble, but time for me to cut to the chase." He removed a pistol from under his jacket.

"What the hell is this?" Her feet slid on a metal door just beneath a pile of leaves and she stumbled backward as he advanced on her.

"Plan B."

He grabbed her arm, then snarled. "Give me your gun. I know you have one, and don't make any sudden moves."

"Open it," he demanded, pointing at her feet. "And no funny stuff."

She cleared the leaves under her feet, slid back a rusty latch, and pulled the handle, revealing a set of steps.

"This is going to hurt a bit," he warned.

When Amara spun around, the handle of the weapon struck her in the face. Her knees buckled, and Jarul tossed her over his shoulder and descended the stairs. She floated in and out of consciousness as he zip-tied her hands and feet together, then taped her mouth shut.

I've come too far to die like this.

She lifted her head to try and familiarize herself with her surroundings, but the darkness closed in on her. She fought back the urge to cry. That's what weak females did, and she was a warrior and a true avenger. After coming this far, she wouldn't be stopped by a traitor motivated by greed.

* * *

"What happened to Ivy," Naysa asked, watching Luiza pour a triple portion of Tito's into a crystal glass.

"She killed Robert," Ian said, swiping several screens on his cell.

"And, Ezra Davidson, his grandfather," Luiza added. She took several sips of the clear concoction. "Then Ivy had the nerve to go to court and request custody of the children. Citing the fact that since they no longer had a father, she was all they had left."

Ian whistled. "She had some nerve."

"You don't know the half of it," Luiza said.

"I'm still confused as to what this has to do with everything?" he said.

"The letters and fragrance all point to Ivy." What she could never voice out loud, not even to herself was the fear lingering in the pit of her stomach of 'what if'. What if Robert didn't die? And all this time, she was fearful it could be his ex-wife wreaking havoc on her sanity but all along, it was Robert returning to torture her.

In all that she had shared with her therapist and daughter, one thing she kept hidden was a secret so dark, she hadn't yet spoken the words out loud.

"Do you think it was her?" Ian asked. "After all, she has been released from prison."

"Or there is a copy—" she stopped midsentence. "What do you mean, 'She's been released from jail?' How would you know that?"

Ian's gaze cut to Naysa, who turned the other way. He remained silent as he added more logs to the fire and stoked the flames until they roared.

"If my dad and grandfather were shot and killed, and you paralyzed," Naysa asked. "How were they caught?"

The wood crackled, sending sparks onto the floor. Ian quickly stamped them out.

"Benjamin went to his neighborhood pool hall, and after getting sloshed, started running his mouth. At the table next to him was an off-duty cop. He later testified that the discussion about camping out in the ex-husband's backyard in wait to kill, sounded too strange to be fictional so he called it in."

"Wait, are you saying she actually hid in his backyard?" Ian asked.

"This is where it gets hinky," she said. "Police found a tent, used adult diapers, and pre-packaged food, along with Ivy's DNA."

"Wow, so the entire incident was premeditated?" Naysa asked.

"Everything except her father getting drunk and spilling his guts in a bar."

Chapter 26

Amara regained consciousness and found her hands, feet, and mouth bound. Sweat poured from her brow and stung her eyes. She contorted her lean body and twisted her wrists downward until she heard her joints crack. Forcing herself not to panic, Amara wriggled through the loop her bound arms created.

In agony, she tugged at the zip ties until they cut through her flesh. The blood provided the friction she needed to force her hands through the opening of the ties. Once free, she reached into her boot. Locating the hunting knife, she cut the ties from around her feet.

"Rule number one," she said as soon as she ripped the tape from her mouth. "Check every inch of your opponent before subduing them. You never know when they might resurrect."

She retrieved a nickel-plated 38 Special from her right boot. When she stood, her foot landed on something that yielded. A delighted smile crossed her face when she retrieved what turned out to be a discarded book of matches. Amara closed her eyes and imagined she was a child again, navigating through the dark halls and tight spaces of the delipidated building where her family was forced to live following her parent's divorce. Gone were the massive rooms in her dad's house.

Amara and her brother sought entertainment playing in closets and dank basements. She stumbled up the steps of the fallout shelter nursing a massive headache.

Idiot didn't even lock the entrance.

Amara closed her eyes and listened to the stillness. Focus, daughter. What do you hear? West of her, a set of boots trudged through the leaves. She gathered leaves, twigs, and small branches, piled them on the door of the shelter, and set it on fire using matches she had found. Fire and black smoke flared ten feet into the air.

* * *

Luck favored her and the man she now knew was Kennedy. came trotting back toward where he'd left her.

His voice was loud as he spoke into his cell. "Fire in the woods. I'm going to investigate."

From where she hid behind a tree, Ian's commanding tone was clear on the airwaves. He was bringing reinforcements.

Kennedy was almost upon her when he tripped over a log hidden beneath a bed of leaves. He went crashing to the ground, which sent his weapon careening into the field of grass.

Before he could rise, Amara put one foot on his head. "So nice of you to come and check on me."

He struggled to turn over, but she pressed harder on his neck.

"You'll never get away with—"

Finger on the trigger, Amara said, "No time for small talk."

She placed the small handgun at the base of his neck and pulled the trigger twice. Then she retrieved the Maxim 9 and shoved it in her waist. That built-in silencer is a handy feature.

"And this, Jarul or should I say, Kennedy, is Plan C," she whispered in his ear. His vacant eyes stared into the darkness.

After rubbing her hands along the back of his neck, she wiped them on her shirt for dramatic effect, then ran the few hundred yards back towards the cabin. It was time to complete her mission.

"Help me!" she screamed. "Someone, please help me."

Three young guards bolted from the parking lot in front of the cabin. "Where is Jarul?" they shouted once they recognized her.

Panting as if struggling for air, she pointed a bloody finger at the now raging fire. "I don't know," she screamed. "I heard what sounded like gunfire and took off running."

Two of them turned and fanned out to search for Jarul. One stayed at her side. When he looked away, she shot him with Jarul's gun, then the others. Four down, more to go.

She ran across the clearing, up the steps of the cabin, then banged on the front door, screaming. When Ian opened it, she screamed, "Someone is out there, and I couldn't find Jarul!"

Her gut-wrenching wail brought all but Luiza to their feet.

Ian gripped her hands at the wrists and turned them back and forth. "Is this your blood?" he asked.

Marco stepped in closer and focused on her.

"I … I … don't know." She sobbed, making it difficult for Ian to make out anything she was saying.

He barked into the headset, "Everyone, check in, now." Four agents responded then the line went silent. He repeated the order two additional times, which yielded the same results.

Naysa immediately positioned herself at her mother's side, while Ian stood in the center of the room watching Amara.

She dropped her head onto the counter of the bar, and Naysa ran to her. "Amara, please sit."

After handing her a bottle of water, Naysa ran to the sink, snatched several paper towels from the roll and wet them. "Clean your hands."

She returned to soak more paper in cold water and placed one wad on the back of Amara's neck, and the other on her forehead, instructing her to hold them in place.

While Ian continued to yell orders. Amara slowly sipped water,

"Are we just going to remain here like sitting ducks?" Luiza yelled, shaking her head back and forth.

"Finster," Ian said, "what's your location?" Upon hearing the response, "Maintain your position at the front of the cabin. I need you three to secure the perimeter of the cabin until the fire department and the police arrive."

"I'll go locate the others," Marco said, checking his clip for ammunition. "Check one, two," he spoke into the earpiece.

"I hear you loud and clear," Ian said.

"There's a fire," Amara's voice was raspy as she spoke. "Be careful, it looked like it was spreading."

"We need to get out of here," Luiza screamed over Ian's words. "I told you we shouldn't have come here. This place has nothing but pain."

"We're safer in here," Amara said in a cool tone, "than outside with a damn lunatic."

"Everyone," Ian yelled, "be quiet."

Marco held up one finger and went out through the front door in search of Jarul and the other three agents.

Ian bellowed and pointed toward the fireplace. "I need all three of you to be in one area."

"Marco, what do you see?" Ian asked, keeping his eyes trained on Naysa as she sat in a chair next to Luiza, who'd aged ten years over the past five minutes. Lowering his voice, he said, "Luiza, do you need water?"

She shook her head.

Amara opened the refrigerator, reached in, and a couple of items fell out. The sound of plastic bottles hitting the tile floor instantly made everyone jump, except Ian.

"Let me help you?" Naysa grabbed several towels from the counter and began wiping up the spilled water. "Are you alright? You're shivering."

"I'm fine. Just a little cold from being outside." Amara avoided her gaze and walked over to the fireplace, rubbing up and down her arms.

Chapter 27

"Naysa," Luiza said, casting an anxious glance her way. "You have been awfully quiet. What's on your mind?"

"I know, Mother …" she said, biting down on her bottom lip. A tear spilled from her eye.

"You know what?" Luiza said.

"I know that my father beat you."

Luiza gasped, pulling the attention of everyone in the room.

"I don't know what you think you know." Luiza's words were harsh and filled with resentment. "But you don't know anything of the sort." Sniffing the air, she added, "And why am I still smelling that disgusting fragrance?"

"This is not the time or the place to be talking about any of this," Amara said, running her hand through her hair. She deeply inhaled her wrist.

"It's as good a time as any," Naysa insisted, "especially since we don't know what the hell is happening right now."

Naysa's face was etched in unspeakable pain. Each line screamed countless nights of horror. The stack of police reports, hospital records, the ultrasound of the stillborn baby boy who, according to the report, said she fell down a flight of stairs all testified to the unmentionable pain her mother endured in silence.

"I know," Naysa whispered, not giving up her position. "I read the complete trial summary."

When a knock sounded at the door, Ian drew his weapon before answering.

"We have a problem," Finkel said in a hushed tone, then passed him a thin wallet. "This was found in the back seat of one of the vehicles."

Ian flipped the wallet open and released a soft curse when he held it closer.

"Tell everyone to spread out and find them," he bellowed as Finkel left. Turning back into the room, he said, "Luiza, change in plans."

"Ian!"

The scream startled him.

Now, Amara stood next to Luiza with a gun flush against her temple.

"What the hell are you doing, Amara?" Naysa yelled; the harsh sound of her voice foreign to her own ears.

"Always one for questions, aren't you?" Her tone was abrasive as her gaze shot to Ian. "This time, you're not in charge, so put your weapon on that counter and sit your ass down, or I'll be adding more blood to what you already see."

Ian placed his gun on the island then raised both hands in the air, palms facing her.

"None of that hostage negotiation shit either," she said. "There'll be no concessions."

He didn't speak but held his position.

"Big man," she said. "Perhaps this will entice you to take heed to my words." With the butt-end of the weapon, she struck Luiza in the head. If Amara wanted the satisfaction of hearing her cry, it went unfulfilled. Luiza never flinched.

"Mother," Naysa screamed, running in her direction.

"Don't take another step," Amara said. "Do what you do best, nothing. For the record, the name isn't Amara, though I've felt very bitter." She laughed at that as if it were a joke. "My name is Sophia."

Naysa's mouth opened, but no words came out.

"Why am I doing this, you might wonder?" She scanned their faces, her eyes glinting with malice. "Take a look and tell me who I resemble." Wriggling her eyebrows in a demented fashion she added, "I was always told I favored my father and was Daddy's little princess."

Naysa frowned and exchanged a puzzled look with Ian, then a comment a staff member had made about Amara and her came to memory, and she gasped.

"I take it you see the similarities. Yes, I'm Robert's daughter." This time, she chuckled. "That line sounded so much better when James Earl Jones said it to Luke Skywalker. Anyway, when I left, Luiza was sharing how she broke up my mom and dad's happy marriage." She forced the muzzle closer to Luiza's head, breaking the skin. Blood slowly dripped down her face and onto the fabric of her dress.

"I did not break up their marriage. Your parents were separated when I met him," Luiza said in a matter-of-fact tone.

"So now you want to use your inside voice. That's more than fine with me." Looking at Ian, she said, "Did she tell you how after my mother was locked up, my grandpa Ezra had a heart attack? Or that my brother committed suicide?"

"Amara," Ian said, "I think this has gone far enough. Let's end this right now."

Luiza jerked her head. "You can't blame that on me, Amara."

"I told you, my name is Sophia."

"Sophia," she corrected, taking shallow breaths. "I didn't know about your brother. I'm so sorry."

"Like hell you are. You only cared about getting in my daddy's bed and into his bank account." Amara screamed, while toying with the necklace she wore. "You didn't care anything about my family or me."

"Who do you think gave you that?" Luiza peered closely at Amara's chest, then tilted her head as if she'd had a revelation. "I placed that necklace around your neck when you were just three years old. That was me."

"Liar!" Amara shrilled.

"Look at it closely. You have the exact one as mine and Naysa's. I had hers designed after ours."

Naysa reached inside her blouse and revealed a matching necklace.

"You're trying to trick me. I know it." Staring at Ian as he shifted his body weight, she taunted him. "Try me."

"All you had to do," she said, pointing to Naysa. "Was allow the new port to go through smoothly, and once the reef died off, I would've exposed you and claimed all that was mine. Not even a road accident could kill you. That BMW was supposed to ensure that was your last day on planet Earth."

Large cinders broke off and tumbled onto the floor and carpet.

"Don't you dare move," she seethed. "A little fire never hurt no damn body …" She wiped one hand across her mouth, spreading saliva from her lips to her cheek.

"I'm already dead. I died the day my parents' marriage dissolved."

"Why did you leave the letter?" Ian asked, now standing with both hands behind him.

"As if the answer will do you any good." She continued ranting, "I knew Jarul would eventually put the pieces of the puzzle together. He had articles on his desk about the triple murders."

"What does Jarul have to do with this?" Ian asked.

"I guess your background checks didn't catch everything," Amara snorted as she spoke. "He flipped on you. He was burning both ends against the middle. Moscow knows him as Kennedy Kowalsky. I know him as dead."

"You killed him?" Ian's eyes hardened. "Did you also kill Thunderstorm?

"Why was she murdered?" Naysa yelled. "She never hurt anyone."

"I wish I could take credit for that, but it was Jarul, Kennedy, whatever the hell his name was. Ironically, he gave me the idea to extort Luiza. He developed the idea for the port and to divert tourist money from the main island to his benefactors. But like everyone else, he got greedy."

"What about the packages, including the fake bomb? Were you a part of that?" Ian asked.

Wearing an evil smile, Amara said, "Maybe I was and maybe I wasn't."

The rug caught fire, and bands of smoke circled their feet.

"Isn't this cozy." A rabid smile spread across Amara's face. "We all get to watch each other die."

As more smoke filled the room, Luiza slowly winked at Ian, and he nodded.

Amara turned her head from Ian to Luiza then back again.

"Amar … I mean, Sophia," Naysa held her gaze. "Your mother has been released from jail. Did you know that?"

"Stap yuh rass." Amara blinked several times as the meaning of her words reverberated in Naysa's head. Stop talking shit.

"It's true," Naysa said, inching closer as she spoke. "She was allowed to go home several weeks ago. Has she tried to contact you?"

"You're lying," Amara pointed the gun in Naysa's direction as she shouted. "Sit the fuck down. My mother would never be free and not come to look for—"

"Game over," Luiza snarled as she jammed a hunting knife deep into Amara's thigh.

When she yelped in pain, Ian shot her twice in the chest.

Amara was dead before she collapsed to the floor.

Leaning forward, Luiza wiped the blood off the blade onto Amara's blouse then returned it to the side pocket of the wheelchair.

Finster raced into the room, sweeping the area with his weapon. "I heard gunshots," he shouted.

"The situation is under control." Ian lunged towards Amara's corpse and kicked away the gun that fell from her hand as a log splintered on the wooden floor and antique carpet. Bright orange flames licked greedily at the Persian rug.

Finster surveyed the room then grabbed a fire extinguisher from the wall above the stove.

"There's a second one in the closet over there." Naysa pointed, then quickly wheeled Luiza outside to safety.

The two men wielded the extinguishers in wide arcs to bring the fire under control before backing out of the cabin to join the others in the yard. Dust and flashing lights filled the air as several vehicles sped up the gravel driveway towards the cabin.

Naysa took deep breaths and swiped tears from her eyes, thankful the people who mattered to her were safe and sound.

"Since the cavalry is here," Luiza said, wearing a lopsided smile. "Take my ass home."

Chapter 28

Seven months later …

Naysa opened her eyes to find Ian's hand resting comfortably atop her swollen belly.

"Good morning." He kissed her on her cheek. "Take your time dressing. Everyone is in the dining room."

When he left, Naysa stretched and got out of bed. The baby moved, and she softly stroked her belly. Aria and Liam had been ecstatic over the news that they would soon have a new brother or sister. They had already been to Belize once since Naysa's visit to their home, and Ian was trying to gain permanent custody of them, given his ex-wife's mental instability and recent shenanigans.

On her night table, an envelope caught her eye. She recognized the handwriting immediately. It was from Marco. Knowing his resourceful nature, she didn't question how the note had gotten there.

It was great seeing you, if only for a brief amount of time. You look amazingly happy. I'd always hoped it would be me who'd be responsible for a wide grin upon your face, but I see someone has beat me to it. Well, not really beat me. Because we both know the special place I hold in your heart.

I am always just a call away. Go easy on your new husband. Ian isn't as tough as he pretends. He has a genuine love for you. He's your best asset. Take care and I'll always love you. I'm here if things don't work, or better yet, if they do.

The drama at the cabin still made her head spin. In the process of identifying the bodies found on the grounds after Sophia's attack, Ian realized Jarul wasn't who they thought he was. When Audley, the previous guard, was eventually found dead in a swamp, Ian was certain an opening had been created for Jarul to slip into their team.

Ian had fired the local tech guru and slapped charges on him after he admitted to tampering with their software and creating a profile for Jarul that would pass inspection when he turned up for an interview.

As Luiza had quipped, the trash around them had been taken out in one sweep.

* * *

Thirty minutes later, Naysa walked into the dining room to the smell of fresh coffee, bacon, maple syrup, and the sound of applause. "What is this?" she asked, blushing at the sight of the group of men all clad in expensive suits.

Xavier stood patiently at the serving table.

"Good morning," Naysa said, touching his shoulder as she walked to Ian's side.

Grant shook Ian's hand. "Thank you for protecting them."

"Oh, hell," Luiza said. "Don't get all mushy on us now."

"The Kings have spoken," Khalil said, the expression of pride fully visible on his face. "By unanimous decision, we have appointed you to have oversight of the island of Belize in terms of our philanthropy projects and the work you are doing for women trapped in dangerous situations."

Naysa stood speechless for a few moments. Her mind went back to the distant past …

"Papa Khalil," her voice squeaked as she spoke. "When I'm on my throne," she said. "I'm gonna be a great girl King."

"That's awesome, sweetie," Khalil said, kissing her on the top of her head. "You are going to make a great queen. Until then, you can be my lil Princess."

She marched around the room. "This is how I wave, Papa Khalil?" she moved her hand from left to right, smiling brightly as she marched around his chair.

"One day," he said with a bright smile. "You're going to make a phenomenal queen."

"Did you hear that, Naysa?" Ian said.

"And what might that be?" she asked.

"The sound of the bag exploding from around that darn cat. It's finally out in the open."

"Good morning, Queen," everyone said while applauding.

Khalil looked down at his goddaughter with a combination of admiration and affection. "I don't know what I would've done had we lost you."

"I told you," Ian said. "I protect what's mine."

Epilogue

Naysa, Luiza, and Ian traveled along the pathway through the residence's garden. They paused near a cluster of newly planted trees. Luiza dropped an arm around Naysa's waist and her other hand atop her daughter's growing stomach. "Hello, Ian Grant Khalil Richardson," she said.

"Mother, you continue adding names. He'll need two birth certificates."

"But as long as his first name is Ian, you may add as many as you like." Ian stood with his shoulders squared and his chin tilted high, then stepped back to give them a moment of privacy when Naysa handed Luiza the brass engraved plates.

One was meant for each tree: Robert Davidson, Ezra Davidson, Sophia Davidson, Jason Davidson, Rahul Perez, Thunderstorm Artist, Jarul Rusnick.

Her mother paused as she viewed the names.

"We cannot solely judge people on their bad actions," Naysa said. "Jarul or Kennedy, was a part of our family even if he was only here for a short time."

Luiza nodded, conscious that her puckered lips hinted at her displeasure.

"I felt so close to her," Naysa said, swiping a tear from her eyes. "If only she'd told me who she was, we could have had a beautiful relationship."

"Amara couldn't see past her jealousy and hatred," Luiza said.

Luiza patted her hand. "Are you ready for your big announcement regarding A Place to Ponder?"

"Thunderstorm would be so excited to see how far the work has progressed with the reefs," Naysa said. "Soon, it will be nearly impossible to see any signs of destruction."

Luiza nodded. "And that would have been what she wanted, to see her life's work come to fruition."

In the intervening months, Naysa had several meetings with the hoteliers and the port authority. They had arrived at mutually beneficially terms on which they could all co-exist, including tours of the reefs for hotel guests and sizeable donations toward its preservation.

Ian quietly walked up behind them. "Queen, we must meet with the press in just a few moments. Adrian Rodriguez will be arriving momentarily."

Slipping her hand into his and kissing his cheek, she said, "I'm as ready as I'll ever be."

About the Author

Aiken Ponder grew up admiring authors that wielded their pens like a sword. Learning from the masters, she too put pen to paper, clearing her path to success. Aiken writes across many genres, including Erotica, Mysteries, Paranormal, and Adult Contemporary Literature.

Aiken is a member of NK Tribe called Success and Cavalcade of Authors. Her debut book, 80 Days of Pleasure, collaborates with New York Times and USA Today Bestselling Authors. Aiken's books feature powerful women who unapologetically embrace their authenticity and boldly walk in their purpose and passion.

You may follow her on all social media sites under Aiken Ponder.
IG: https://www.instagram.com/aiken_ponder/
Facebook: https://www.facebook.com/AuthorAikenPonder/
Website: www.aikenponder.com

I am so thankful for your support and look forward to reading your reviews.

Queens of the Castle Series

Each Queen book is a standalone, NO cliffhangers

USA TODAY, and National Bestselling Authors have created a world where women can—and will have it all—love, family, career, and leave a legacy while overcoming generational challenges.

These powerful women, brought together for a higher purpose, change lives by providing safety for those who cannot protect themselves; care for those from tragic backgrounds, and make an impact on their families, communities, and the world at large.

The Kings laid the foundation; the Knights created a bridge of hope between continents; but the Queens will change the world.

Queen of Lahaina

Someone is sabotaging Dr. Lani Jamison's career and their tactics are escalating. Are the attacks attempts to prevent Lani from working with The Castle to implement robotic surgery in the hospital? Or does her association with Jordan Spears have his clients seeking to take her out of the picture?

Jordan lives a complicated life from his family dynamics to his "interesting" career. When Lani tries to distance herself from him, he's forced to temporarily accept it as he staves off the hostile demands of his brother who has racked up debt with the criminals who won't take no for an answer. Will Jordan be able to convince Lani that their relationship deserves a chance despite its origins? And will Lani survive an unknown enemy's endeavor to put her six feet under?

Queen of Shadow Bay

Not all monsters are born, some are made.

Killing Carpathia was the first mistake. Informing her niece made it worse. Durabia meant a fresh start for Raye Bennett. One phone call destroyed all of that. Returning to American soil could send her back to prison for the rest of her life. Attending the funeral of a family member may be deadlier. Heaven and Hell change places in this romantic thriller where the poison is sweeter than the wine.

Queen of North Shore

Solange Porter never believed her husband, Emmitt would betray her. But he did. First, he died when he promised they'd be together forever. Then, he left her as the head of a tech company that she didn't want to lead. She wasn't alone; most of the staff felt the same way.

Computer programmer Wale Adisa needs Solange's help. To get it, he will share a secret that Emmitt never revealed to her. This secret will not only increase her feelings of betrayal. It may also place a target on her back that could ruin her and the company she's trying to save.

Queen of Belize

By birth, she is royalty. By choice she is an avenger and equalizer for those who have no voice. When dark forces emerge and threaten not only her queendom but her life, Naysa, Queen of Belize becomes a foot soldier, calling upon the assistance of allies and a few nemeses to help aid in a personal war. It's then that she fulfills the meaning of her name, glorious war hero.

Queen of Kingston

Samantha DaCosta, reporter extraordinaire, stumbles upon an explosive story in her research of several wealthy, humanitarians connected to The Castle, a place reserved for the mega-rich.

Her uncle, who is a member, has invested in a medical facility that produces and distributes vaccines to third-world countries. The medication has deadly adverse effects, which sets up Ted DaCosta as a target for blackmail.

As Sam uncovers disturbing details, she's conflicted. When her personal safety is threatened, she must either pretend not to know the implications of this nefarious plot, or speak up and bring down a hailstorm of publicity. Danger also stalks her to Jamaica in the form of an assassination attempt.

Kingston "King" Coburn is content to support his woman's endeavors, but when work impacts her well-being, he draws the line. Instead of pulling her back from the edge of a dark abyss, he's drawn into the world of power brokers, who will do anything to increase their wealth.

Only the couple's combined skills and access to a safe haven will keep them alive at the end of their harrowing search for the truth.

Queen of Cambridge

Billionaire chocolatier Caressa Sidaná is one of the most recognizable names in the confectionery industry, but she is looking to expand into other ventures. She is shrewd and no-nonsense, but in her pursuit of business dominance, she has made some mistakes along the way, including the oft-clichéd misstep of mixing business with pleasure.

Her expansion efforts lead to a chance meeting with Ishmael Abdur-Hafiz, an international weapons dealer with the type of connections that could prove beneficial for all parties involved. Their intense attraction and mutual business pursuits draw the attention of a former lover-turned-enemy, intent on ruining everything she has built and permanently removing Ishmael from her life.

Can she find a way to deal with the consequences of her decisions and save her company from potential destruction?

Queen of Wilmette

Milan Alessia Jackson battled through the scars left in her life from a contentious relationship. Her grandmother served as her protector and guardian angel until she took her last breath. International lawyer Vikkas Germaine was her childhood friend and true love. Life's circumstances separated them, but his father served as the catalyst to reunite them.

As the couple settle into their new marriage and Durabia, unexpected challenges rise up and threaten to tear their relationship apart. Secrets from her past, an unexpected trip to South Carolina and family members primed to settle scores surface, leading to a whirlwind of upheaval in their lives. Can their love survive these storms or will forces in play destroy everything they're building?

Queen of Curacao

Waking up from a coma—without her memory intact—is not something Cassandra anticipated when she says her goodbyes to her best friend, promising to find her daughter, along with the other children who went missing since the arrival of an unknown criminal organization in Curaçao.

Queen of Bahia

Pilar Silva couldn't have anticipated the danger she would encounter after being forced to return home to Brazil to care for an ailing family member.

She encounters the one person hired to establish the cause of the increased deaths in Bahia. They discover their passions lead to more than an investigation.

PURPOSE

Life According to God's Plan

FLORENZA DENISE LEE

Excerpt from Purpose

Sixteen Years Old - 1980

"Suicide hotline, please hold."

If music played or if I stood there in silence, I cannot recall. What I do remember is my shaking hand cradling the receiver to my ear. The click of being placed on hold was the loudest sound I'd ever heard. I was in total disbelief. To this day, reflecting on that pivotal moment causes my skin to crawl. My vision blurred, then tunneled as my mind spun like a roulette wheel—around and round, it went. Holding my breath, I waited for the little white ball to stop. Secretly, I feared I was about to create a new landing space. If this proved to be accurate, I worried I would not survive.

The plush tan carpet found its way between blue-painted toes as my bare feet teetered on the edge of the first step on the landing. With sweaty palms, I gripped the handrail, fearing my knees might give way as I felt the cream-colored walls pressing in. Finding my voice, and it shook with fear. "Hello, is anyone there?"

Tears stung my eyes as I realized my lifeline had failed me. Yet again, I was left alone.

Fine. If I can't get help, I'll just do it.

It's surprising how determination manifests at the most inopportune time. Just moments prior, I'd lacked the strength to hold a phone to my ear. Yet now, I felt I could lift a car. I punched the disconnect button to end the call and stretched my five-foot three-inch frame as I reasoned within myself. Perhaps they were counseling some other soul who needed assistance. I prayed they'd at least received what I hadn't.

Phone in hand, I counted the eight steps back to the only bathroom in our three-bedroom home. Some might consider it a small house, but to us, it was a palace. Glancing to my right, I saw my brother's bedroom. He was the only boy and always had his own space. For a moment, I thought about tidying it for him but decided otherwise—no time to spare. I was on a mission.

The bedroom that I shared with my two sisters was just a few feet away. Bunkbeds flanked the far wall. A twin-size bed was parallel to it. Bed linen, curtains, throw rugs—nothing matched.

Without even looking underneath the single bed, I knew what was there, well-read books, and many. Each night, I read by the streetlight that flooded through the small window. If I had five cents for every time my mother caught me reading past bedtime, let's just say I'd have a lot of nickels. I'm going to miss my books the most.

I could not silence the woman's voice as it screamed, please hold inside my head, mocking my pain. What I interpreted from her actions was, "Who are you trying to fool? You aren't about to do anything irrational. Stop wasting my time."

"Oh, I'm not, am I? Then watch this." Stomping to the bathroom, I retrieved several bottles from the metal shelves and then lined the contents along the edge of the white porcelain sink. The thought to flush them down the toilet or wash them down the drain left as fast as it entered my mind. Overtaking me was a determination to be destructive.

When they find out I was serious, I bet they'll never place another caller on hold.

If the camel needed a straw to break its back, a call on hold was it.

80 Days of Pleasure

AIKEN PONDER

Prologue

Sarvanti's long-toned legs glistened in the sun as she trotted across the parking lot towards the Buick Cascada. The oversized khaki shorts did little to hide curves that only youth, clean eating, and hours in the gym could create. Although Sarvanti's stunning and statuesque features easily could have landed her on the cover of any fashion magazine, she loved working as a valet. Sarvanti quickly slid her lean frame behind the wheel of luxury cars that many of her male classmates only lied about driving.

Being outside in the fresh air was far better than being cooped up behind a desk, fake smiling at customers while answering phones any day. Just the thought of being trapped in a windowless cubical caused her temples to throb. Singers, athletes, actors, politicians, and such. She learned that if she kept her looks natural, not drawing too much attention to herself, she could get up close and personal. As a journalist student, the stories she overheard could easily make her rich and famous. For right now, she was just a fly on a wall with a very thick notebook.

The lush black leather interior was a stark contrast to the white exterior. The car gleamed from a recent detail and professional waxing.

"Who did you meet today, Vanti?" Her mother's thick Italian accent echoed through her Bluetooth earpiece. She was fascinated with those who achieved the American Dream and always wanted to know which celebrity her daughter rubbed elbows with.

"Someone you'd just die to meet." Sarvanti teased while glancing over her shoulder, ensuring no one was within earshot. "But you'd think with his fame, he'd be endorsed by Mercedes or Maserati."

"Endorsed? He must be very famous? What type of vehicle does he have?" Her mother's voice rose an octave higher. Next to celebrities, she loved automobiles more.

"He's someone you've always wanted to meet," she said. "I can afford this on my salary." Sarvanti spoke into her earpiece as she hit the key fob. Cell phones were not permitted at work, especially while driving.

"If it's who I think it is, please take a photo for me," her mother pleaded in her ear.

"I'm not supposed to, but …" she said as she opened the car door. "I'll try." She glanced around again. "You know I'm not supposed to ask customers for their autographs—" Sarvanti put her foot on the brake pedal then punched the start button. "Besides, he's not alone. He's with a young girl. Maybe it's another one of those charity things he does. You know, take an orphan to lunch or something. Only there are no paparazzi."

"Just try."

"Alright, but if I get fired," she warned. "I'll be moving back in with you. Love you, mom." She tapped her ear, ending the call as she drove the few hundred feet back to the front door.

* * *

"Thank you again for lunch. You didn't have to bring me to such a fancy place." Nova nervously rolled her thumbs together as she looked down at a pair of scuffed shoes and holes forming at the knees of her jeans. She glanced at his plate. "How was the—what's it called again?"

"Cioppino, and it was delicious once they prepared it correctly."

"Well, you sent it back six times," she said, then suddenly added, "I'm sorry. I wasn't trying to be disrespectful. I'd just be scared they'd try to mess with my food afterward."

"You'll learn. You must demand perfection, especially when you're paying. I'm the customer. They're here to serve me." He squared his shoulders and tilted his chin forward. "Besides, I like the way they prepare the shrimp, clams, and mussels. Sending it back prompted them to get their act together." He pushed his dish forward. "You look as if you really enjoyed your meal."

Her eyes cast downward as the heat rose to her cheeks. They matched the carnations in the miniature vase of water on the table. Her plate bore no signs that a healthy portion of lasagna had occupied it a few moments before. The dish that held the crème Brule was even cleaner. Both plates looked as though they had been licked clean. Truthfully, if seated alone, she probably would have. "I would've been happy with either McDonald's or Wendy's. You didn't have to spend so much."

"Nonsense," he said, placing a platinum credit card back into the wallet, then took out cash instead as he stood. "How would it look if I took you to a fast-food greasy burger joint?" He walked around and pulled her chair back, allowing her to stand.

The waitress partially opened the black leather folder with the bills. Her face contorted as she lifted the slip of paper and glanced under it. She mumbled as she slapped the binder closed then turned to walk away.

Pausing, he reached into his pocket, revealing a necklace which he placed around her neck.

She immediately reached up to grasp the small diamond dangling from her throat.

"It isn't fancy," he said. "I didn't want to draw attention to it."

Tears filled her eyes. "It's beautiful."

"Just a little something to remind you I'm always thinking of you." Nova leaned into his hug. Although only thirteen, she was very tall for her age. The top of her head practically reached his shoulder as they walked side by side towards the front door.

"Each place seems to get nicer than the one before," she said softly. "I don't want you to think I'm trynna get stuff from you … I mean, I still can't believe that after all this time, you found me." Tears formed in the inner corners of her eyes. She quickly reached up with a hand and swiped them away. "All my life, I was told no one knew who my dad was." She watched as the valet drove the white convertible towards them. "When my mom died from an overdose of heroin, I went from one home to another home …."

Placing his hand on her chin and tilting her face towards his, "I can only imagine all that you've gone through, and I'm so sorry," he said. "I'm here now, and I'm not going anywhere."

"Some of the things I've gone through were—"

"You don't have to say them. I just need you to have a bit more patience. My assistants are working on getting your documentation in order. It'll all be worth the wait, I promise." He smiled broadly, and it put her at ease. "Did you know I gave you your name?"

"You did?"

He kissed her forehead. "Yes, because I knew instantly, you'd be a star."

"My life is no movie unless you are looking for a horror flick."

Nova closed her eyes, rocking on her heels. The sound of his voice alone was like music to her ears. The lyrics were foreign, and she didn't even care that she didn't know the words. If this was a dream, she didn't ever want to wake up. "Do you mind if I call you daddy?"

As soon as the car came to a stop, he held the door open as she slid behind the passenger seat. "Not at all. As a matter of fact, I insist that you do."

He walked around to the awaiting valet as she held open the door with one hand and her palm out with the other. His six-foot-seven-inch frame instantly filled the entire driver's seat. He pulled the door closed without so much as a thank you or tip. The valet's mouth was still ajar as the car sped off and entered traffic.

Nova glanced in the side mirror, and several flashes nearly blinded her. "People take a lot of photos of you," she said.

"I hate when they do that." He scowled, but it quickly disappeared. "I once snatched someone's phone and threw it to the ground." His head went backward as he laughed. "You should have seen his face when the heel of my shoe smashed the phone. It was priceless."

"But—" Nova thought better than saying anything else. In an article in G-Q Magazine, she'd once read that he welcomed fans asking for autographs and photos. Something about his tone made her keep the thoughts to herself.

"Don't believe everything you read," he snapped as though he had read her mind. Then added in a softer tone, "I like my privacy."

* * *

"Thank you for that enthusiastic round of applause," Mayor Swinson bellowed into the microphone. His broad smile caused his beady brown eyes to become practically invisible behind his full cheeks. "Like you, I too am excited about our visitors and the wonderful program they have begun in our fine city." Cheers and loud clapping erupted again. The mayor joined in by pumping his fist in the air. He then raised his hands, asking everyone to kindly be seated.

"Today, we welcome Dallas Avery and his teammates." Dallas' large palm came down on the mayor's right shoulder, nearly engulfing it completely. "They, along with members of the police, clergy, and national and international corporations, have combined efforts to stop human trafficking. It is my greatest honor to ban together with this wonderful organization." Mayor Swinson stepped to his right as Dallas began speaking into the microphone.

"We're so very honored to be here and to share information regarding our organization, A Place to Ponder. To provide a haven for those trapped in human trafficking, we've partnered with local, international, private, and public entities with one purpose in mind, to protect those who cannot help themselves." He looked to his left, "Adrian Hernandez has more information to share." Dallas stepped to the right of the podium.

"Thank you, Mayor Swinson, my teammates, and you for joining us this afternoon. We're very excited to have a special group of youngsters selected via lottery to attend the *Banquet with a Ball Player* yearly event. Each of them will have the opportunity to sit down and eat with several of us and share their story." He applauded in their direction. One teen with braids and a toothy grin waved enthusiastically. "Every year, millions of vulnerable children and women are trafficked for sex around the world. The perpetrator hunts for those who're most vulnerable and then cunningly gains the victim's trust. The nightmare of sex trafficking thrives when law enforcement cannot or does not protect vulnerable children and women." Heads nodded, some women in the audience gasped. "Together with law enforcement, we aim to make it difficult for these punks to profit from selling children and adults caught in their traps. They will know we are hot on their trails."

Cheers and applause erupted from the audience.